Special Message

SOME PAGES IN THIS BOOK ARE FOR YOUR OWN SUPER GOOD SKILLS (Drawing, doodling, quizzes etc...)

Scholastic Children's Books
An imprint of Scholastic Ltd
Euston House, 24 Eversholt Street, London, NW1 1DB, UK
Registered office: Westfield Road, Southam, Warwickshire, CV47 0RA
SCHOLASTIC and associated logos are trademarks and/or
registered trademarks of Scholastic Inc.

First published in the UK by Scholastic Ltd, 2016
This edition published 2017

Copyright © Liz Pichon Ltd, 2016

The right of Liz Pichon to be identified as the author and
illustrator of this work has been asserted by her.

ISBN 978 1407 17748 9

A CIP catalogue record for this book
is available from the British Library.

Printed by CPI Group (UK) Ltd, Croydon, CR0 4YY
Papers used by Scholastic Children's Books are made
from wood grown in sustainable forests.

13

This is a work of fiction. Names, characters, places, incidents and dialogues are products of
the author's imagination or are used fictitiously. Any resemblance to actual people,
living or dead, events or locales is entirely coincidental.

www.scholastic.co.uk

I HOPE you are paying attention.

THANK YOU

To all the **SUPER GOOD** skilled Scholastic team for your **FANTASTIC** support and enthusiasm as EVER. x

HEY!

Pip, Chris, Jude, Kit Rory and Thea. This book's dedicated to YOU! (Keep spreading the T.G. word!)

Special thanks to Georgina too. x

ALL THE SPECIAL ACTIVITY PAGES HAVE BORDERS LIKE [THIS]
So YOU KNOW which ones to LOOK our for.

Contents

Pages for YOU

Mr Fullerman has been in a surprisingly gloomy mood this week. I don't know why. You'd think he'd be HAPPY, ☺ as it's almost the end of TERM.

Mr Fullerman being gloomy

I KNOW I AM!

Yippee!

(My nearly end-of-term leap of joy!)

Mr Fullerman keeps SIGHING and frowning and then saying things like:

Which part of SIT DOWN do you NOT understand?

PLEASE *PUSH* your chairs in. DON'T SCRAPE them...

SIGH...

NO balancing books on heads.

Pens are for writing and drawing. WHAT ARE THEY FOR...?

I *think* Mr Fullerman was EXPECTING us all to say ...

> WRITING AND DRAWING, SIR.

But Brad Galloway  decided they made EXCELLENT drumsticks as well and demonstrated with a spectacular drum roll on his desk.

"PUT THE PENS DOWN, Brad"

So he did ... but not in a sensible way.

The pens went FLYING through the air and narrowly missed Amber, Leroy ...

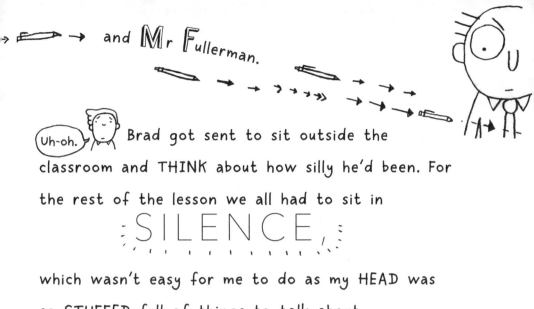

→ ▭ → and Mr Fullerman.

Uh-oh. Brad got sent to sit outside the classroom and THINK about how silly he'd been. For the rest of the lesson we all had to sit in

SILENCE

which wasn't easy for me to do as my HEAD was so STUFFED full of things to talk about.

It was even HARDER to concentrate as Brad kept appearing at the door when Mr Fullerman wasn't looking. I tried not to laugh but Mr Fullerman's FACE wasn't helping. It gave me an idea for some drawings...

Which was a LOT more entertaining than doing my worksheets, that's for sure. Fill in your own messages...

BREAK TIME: ➡

 Derek's already waiting for me. We have to finish a VERY important conversation from this morning about a **BIG** decision.

When I see Derek, straight away I ask him,

 "Have you made up your mind yet?"

"**N**o, I can't decide WHAT to do. It's tricky to choose."

 "We need to sort it out soon. This is important."

"**I** know, I know. I wish we had MORE time!"

As we're discussing WHAT to do, more of our friends come over.

"That sounds SERIOUS," Solid says.

"It IS serious – it could be the difference between having a GOOD band practice and a TERRIBLE one."

Norman hears the words BAND PRACTICE and looks UP.

I haven't missed a
BAND PRACTICE, have I?

"No – sorry, Norman, we haven't had a chance to talk to you about anything yet."

"We need to decide on something really IMPORTANT," I add dramatically.

While I'm TRYING to think of the best way to tell Norman, Marcus butts in.

"What are you two going on about?"

"**I**f YOU had to make this decision,

Marcus, you'd be exactly the same."

(He'd probably be a lot WORSE.)

"**W**e might be able to help you if you tell us,"

Solid says.

 "**G**o on!" Florence calls out.

"We have to choose SOMETHING,"

Derek explains.

"**CHOOSE WHAT?**"

 "Calm down, Marcus. We have to..."

PPPPPPPEEEEEEEEEPPPP!

Mr **S**procket BLOWS the whistle for

end of break.

"**H**URRY UP!" Marcus shouts.

"OK! We HAVE to decide..."

WHAT FLAVOUR CRUNCHY ALIEN SNACKS to have at our BAND PRACTICE.

"IS that IT?" Marcus walks off in a **huff** like we've wasted his time.

AMY and Florence are pulling faces too.

Norman says, "**PHEW!** I thought you might want a NEW drummer!"

Sigh...

"**No way!**" I assure him.

(11)

"It's SERIOUS. Remember when the ONLY snack we had was a packet of **DEAD FLY BISCUITS * ?**" I remind Derek and Norman.

"HOW could we forget? WORST BAND PRACTICE EVER," Derek shudders.

"Even I don't like those biscuits," Norman agrees.

Yuck!

F L A S H B A C K

Dead fly biscuits
(don't contain dead flies)

BEFORE

AFTER

I *think* everyone understands why choosing the right snack is so important now.

*"Dead fly biscuits" are what Granddad Bob calls Garibaldi biscuits because the little currants sandwiched in-between them look a bit like dead flies.

Everyone apart from AMY, who still thinks my snack dilemma is stupid. I KNOW this because when I sit down in class, she tells me.

"Honestly, who gets *THAT* worked up about what flavour SNACK to have? It's NUTS!"

"Crisps, actually – Crunchy Alien ones," I say, trying to make a JOKE. ☺

"Hilarious," AMY says, but not in a FUNNY way.

I should probably just <u>stop</u> talking about the snacks and keep my mouth SHUT. But for some reason I don't.

"The problem is I really like the CHEESY FEET flavour ALIEN snacks – you know, the ones shaped like MASSIVE FEET."

"But Derek likes the pickled onion flavour. AND now we've found out about two new flavours - smoky chicken, and a very interesting-sounding CHIP and KETCHUP: flavour that COULD be amazing, but we don't know YET because we haven't had a chance to try them."

"They all sound DISGUSTING," AMY tells me, pulling a face.

"CHEESY feet flavour SOUNDS disgusting, but they're actually delicious," I point out.

"My Mum hardly EVER asks what snacks we want, so I don't want to miss out. Do you see why it's SO important now?"

"Not really."
(Awkward silence...)

I'm trying to think of something else to say when AMY asks ME a question.

"Tom, is your band still called ?"

"Do you practise a lot, then?"

"LOADS. If you want to be the

band in the world - like we do - it's important."

(I may have exaggerated a bit.)

"When's your next band practice then?"

"Oh! Ummmmmm... I don't know yet."

"I thought you said you practised all the time?"

"We do... We'll probably get together this week."

 "At least the snacks are sorted."

"EXACTLY!"

Marcus leans back in his chair and tries to tell

AMY that **DOGZOMBIES** are a

RUBBISH band.

Rubbish
band

I ignore him and take out my **school planner**. Then in a very organized and sensible way I WRITE in BIG letters, hoping that AMY will see what I've written.

URGENT AND VERY IMPORTANT.

ARRANGE DAY FOR BAND PRACTICE.
(FAR more important than snacks.)

Go for CHEESY FEET and PICKLED ONION flavour.
(I add that last bit in tiny letters underneath.)

THERE, I've made a decision.

All done now.

THE END.

I don't have to THINK about snacks at all any more.

(Well ... maybe just a little bit.)

IMAGINE what other SNACKS and flavours there could be!

What's in the bowl?

Crispy star and cheese nibbles

Spicy alien?

Salt and Onion shells

Chocolate-covered worms with sprinkles

YUM

Sausage and SOCK flavour

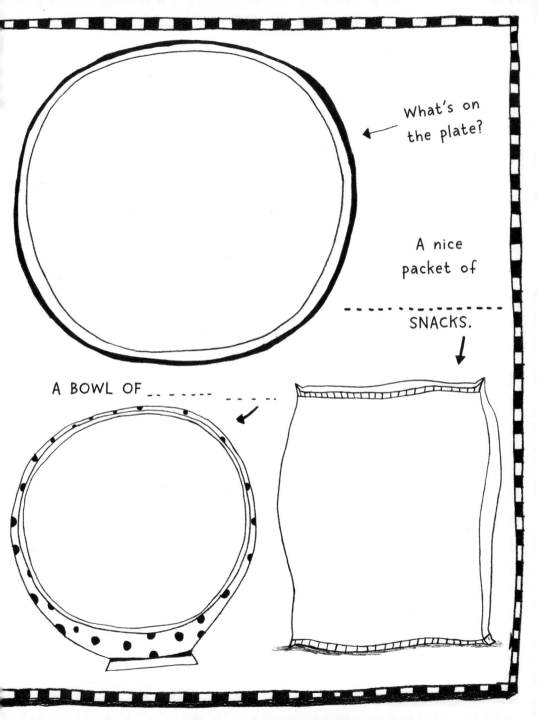

What's on the plate?

A nice packet of

SNACKS.

A BOWL OF _ _ _ _ _ _ _

MORE SPACE FOR MAKING UP YOUR OWN SNACKS!
(Go on, you know you want to.)

Sometimes when Mr Fullerman comes back from break, if he's had a nice cup of tea and a biscuit, he can be all friendly and jolly and look like this:

But not today. ⟹

"**SIT** down, and no more playing with pens, ✎ **BRAD. That goes for ALL of you**," he says in a really STERN voice. "**NOW, as there's only one more day left of school, I have something ELSE planned.**"

A murmur goes around as we think, HOORAY! At LAST something FUN to do.

TODAY we're playing FUN GAMES!

YES!

But that doesn't last long.

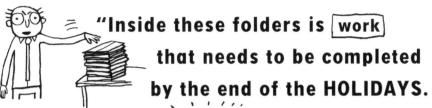

"Inside these folders is [work] that needs to be completed by the end of the HOLIDAYS. IF your folder is empty, GIVE yourself a PAT on the back."

I look over to Marcus Meldrew who starts doing some kind of **WEIRD** dance.

"WHY are you doing that?" I ask.

"I've done all MY work so I'm giving myself a pat on the back."

He stops when Mr Fullerman hands him a folder stuffed with paper.

"This needs to be finished, Marcus."

Huh?

"BUT, SIR!"

"NO **BUTS!**" Mr Fullerman says.

Some kids start laughing because Mr Fullerman has just said the word BUTS REALLY loudly.

He! He! He! Ha! Ha! Ha ... he he...

He!
He!

A FULL-ON BEADY-EYED GLARE ⊙⊙ puts a stop to that pretty fast. Marcus is REALLY fed up. You can tell from his FACE what he's thinking – which gives me another IDEA for some drawings...

So I do these...

Mr Fullerman has been walking around the class handing out folders, but there's nothing for me YET.

I carry on with my game until suddenly he's standing in front of ME and holding up another FOLDER.

"YOU'RE one of the few people with NO work to finish at all," Mr Fullerman tells me.

WOW! That's GOOD.

I was SURE I had some stuff left to do. But I'm not going to ARGUE with Mr Fullerman. To make sure Marcus can hear me, I make a BIG point of saying LOUDLY,

"Thanks, sir. I tried my best. Does that mean I get to do ☆FUN☆ things now?"

"Sorry, Tom, I'm NOT talking to you. This is Amy's folder. Here's yours – it's quite full."

Full

Oh ... so it is.

I have so many bits of work I haven't finished that they spill

out EVERYWHERE.

"YOU have even more than I do!" Marcus says, LAUGHING.

"WELL DONE, AMY! You two need to get on with it,"

Mr Fullerman says, tapping the table.

"HOW do you always get your work done on time?" I ask AMY, who just shrugs her shoulders like it's the easiest thing in the WORLD. (It so isn't.)

"I use my school planner and write things down. Then when I've finished, I tick them off my list."

"You have a LIST?"

"Errrrrr, yes. Just to make sure I don't forget any homework."

"Woah..." I mutter.

She shows me her school planner and how she writes things down.

It's all VERY impressive.

My planner doesn't look anything like that.

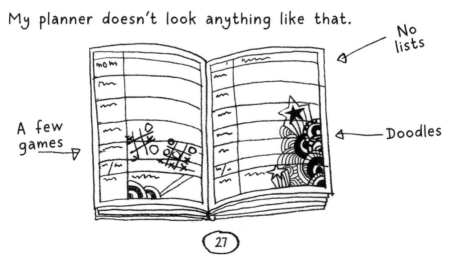

No lists

A few games

Doodles

I flick through the pages to where my holiday dates are. Then I show **AMY** what I normally do to get my homework done. (Not much.)

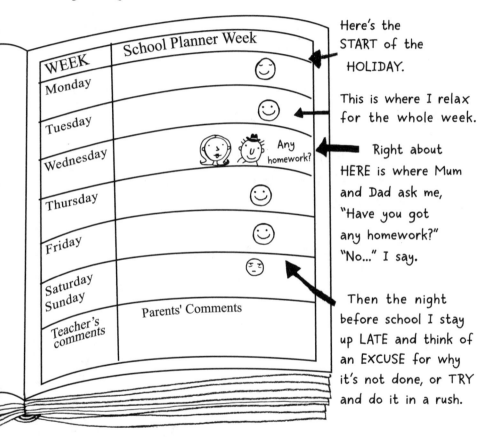

Here's the START of the HOLIDAY.

This is where I relax for the whole week.

Right about HERE is where Mum and Dad ask me, "Have you got any homework?" "No..." I say.

Then the night before school I stay up LATE and think of an EXCUSE for why it's not done, or TRY and do it in a rush.

THAT happens EVERY time. 😞
I draw **AMY** a picture, which explains a bit more.

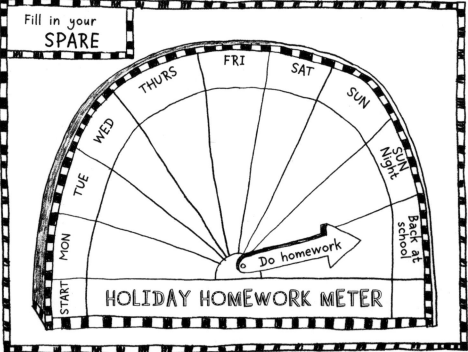

"Sometimes I PANIC and think of an excuse at the same time."
I do an impression, which makes AMY LAUGH.

"No, REALLY, that's what I do."

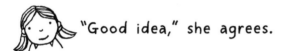 "Oh, I thought you were joking."

"I'm going to write a LIST like YOU do to help me get EVERYTHING done," I whisper to AMY.

"Good idea," she agrees.

I start thinking about my LIST.

What would be REALLY helpful? Hmmm...

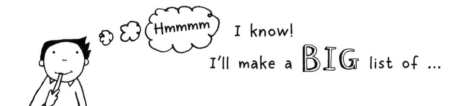 Hmmmm I know!

I'll make a BIG list of ...

HOMEWORK EXCUSES.

I can LOOK at my list if I need one in a HURRY.

★ One STAR - means I've already used it.

★ ★ TWO stars - means I could RISK using it again.

★ ★ The dog ate my homework	
★ The dog buried my homework	
★ The CAT chewed my homework The cat sat on my homework The cat slept on my homework (These can be cats or dogs...)	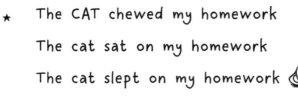
★ The dog STOLE my homework	
★ ★ <u>Dad</u> washed my homework	
★ ★ My homework got soaked by rain	
★ I discovered that MY SISTER is an ALIEN and was too surprised to do homework	

MAKE YOUR OWN HOMEWORK EXCUSE LIST

AMY has been looking over my shoulder.

"Is **THAT** your list?"

"It's ONE of my lists. I'm going to do a HOMEWORK list as well."

(Maybe.)

"Did you really tell **Mr Fullerman** that your sister was an **ALIEN?**"

"Have you SEEN my sister? It could be true."

"I remember when you said your bag got stuck in a TREE," **AMY** reminds me.

"I'd forgotten about that one."
I add it to the list (with two stars). ★ ★

While I'm trying to think of MORE excuses ...

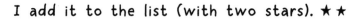

Mr Fullerman is SUDDENLY STANDING behind me. I'm CONVINCED that teachers have lessons on how to SNEAK around the classroom, because one minute **Mr Fullerman** is sitting at his desk and the next ============== he's HERE, and I didn't see or hear him at all.

I think my <u>NINJA</u> skills are quite good, but **Mr Fullerman's** are off the SCALE. **"That's an interesting LIST, Tom,"** he says before I have a chance to cover it UP.

(Uh-oh!)

"I'm writing down IDEAS for my story, sir," I say in a QUICK-thinking kind of way.

"Oh, I see! Homework excuses are part of your story? I'll be looking forward to reading it, Tom. It sounds VERY interesting."

"It will be, sir," I mumble.

Oh, great. Now I'll have to fit one of my excuses into the story. I'll do my best but it isn't going to be easy...

My Sister Is An ALIEN

(True).

BY Tom Gates (who isn't an alien).

There I was, on my way to school and minding my own business. I'd done my homework on time (as always), and it was safely in my bag ready to give to my teacher. Then **SUDDENLY** there was a **BRIGHT LIGHT** in the sky. Me→ I closed my eyes at first and then squinted as the light hovered above me.

WHAT COULD IT BE? I thought (as you would).

Was it a BIRD?
Was it a PLANE?
NO - it was a UFO!

(That's Unidentified Flying Object, in case you didn't know).

Was I really 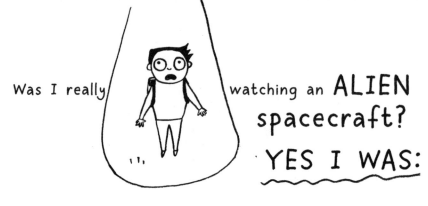 watching an ALIEN spacecraft? YES I WAS:

because it only went and LANDED right in front of me (which was a SHOCK, I can tell you).

I stood very still and watched as the doors began to slowly open. It reminded me of when Granddad Bob YAWNS. ──▶ Yawn...

Then, from out of the darkness inside the spaceship, a small green alien with one eye and one leg appeared and started hopping towards me.

The alien looked me up and down and said, "Take me to your SISTER."

(Which I really wasn't expecting.)

So just to make sure I hadn't misheard the alien, I asked, "Do you mean Delia?"

And the alien said, That's right.

I'd ALWAYS had my suspicions about Delia

←(i.e. - wearing sunglasses all the time and generally being WEIRD).

But HERE was the PROOF that Delia really was an alien.

THEN I started to wonder WHY the alien wanted to see my sister?

So I asked it a QUESTION.

"IF I do tell you where she is, what will you do?" And the alien answered,

"Delia will teach us the ways of humans so we can INVADE and TAKE over your planet."

Which seemed a bit WRONG to me.

After all, Delia might be an ALIEN but she was still my weird sister.

She wouldn't want our planet invaded, I'm sure.

I HAD to think of a PLAN QUICKLY.

 A really good one that would

SAVE the world and maybe

even Delia too.

It was a LOT of pressure.

BUT I DID it.

"You are VERY LUCKY - EVERYTHING

you NEED to know about humans I have

written down in a SECRET document in my

bag. Delia helped me.

You can TAKE it NOW - if you leave her

alone."

The alien thought for a moment and said,

"Hmmmm...

Nice try, human boy."

So I added,

"I'll throw in a packet of WAFERS as well -

they're delicious and humans LOVE them."

WHICH SEALED THE DEAL.

39

I handed over my school bag - the alien took the lot and couldn't FLY away ═══ FAST enough.

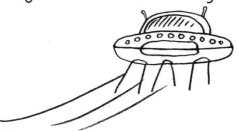

There was only ONE problem now - I was LATE for school and no longer had my homework.

I tried to explain to my teacher what had happened, but he wasn't very impressed.

Really Tom?

(Not really Mr Fullerman)

"But, SIR, it's TRuE - my homework was taken by an alien. I GAVE it up to save the world and my alien sister!"

Which I admit, did sound a little

≷DRAMATIC≷ But I knew the TRUTH.

And now YOU do too.

THE END

40

YIPPEE! ALL DONE. Time for some drawing.
Draw an alien of your own.

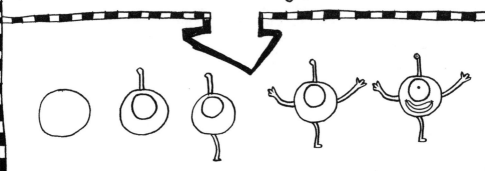

I glance up to make sure Mr Fullerman is still at his desk (he is). It's becoming VERY clear that he has NO plans at all to do anything *FUN*.

(That last worksheet could be it.) 😕

Normally I'd be REALLY fed up about that, but at the moment on a scale of being fed up, I'm only about here. Which is not bad.

THAT'S because for the first time in AGES I have something ELSE to look forward to.
In a few days' time

 I'M GOING ON

That HOLIDAY! doodle took
a while to draw...

... I'm hungry now.

I am **SO** ready to eat that, when the bell goes for lunch, I QUICKLY grab my bag and get out as *fast* as I can.

Ding! Ding!

Ding! Ding!

But then I go and **scrape** my chair when I push it OUT ... and back in. Mr Fullerman calls me back and makes me do it again ➘

QUIETLY...

scrape scrape scrape

scrape scrape

It takes me TWO more goes.

By the time I get down to lunch the queue is **HUGE**. Then I remember I have a packed LUNCH, so I go and join Solid and a few other kids in my class. **But** before I can EAT I have to do something

VERY IMPORTANT. ➡

A LUNCH BOX

INSPECTION

This is to make sure there's nothing unusual **LURKING** inside. FIRST of all I:

1. OPEN my lunch box carefully.

2. Check it **smells** OK.

3. LOOK OUT for any of the following:

odd vegetables **WEIRD** fruit →

 Unidentifiable sandwich fillings

Notes from MUM
Love you Tom X ♥

Anything Delia has added ↓

So far mine looks OK. Bringing **strange** food into school is NEVER a good idea if you ask me, because it always attracts FAR too much attention.

(Not in a good way.)

This is what happened

LAST WEEK.

I was sitting near Florence who brought out some kind of small fruit that I'd never seen before. The skin was a dark reddish colour, and it was all **hard** and **lumpy**. But then she went and peeled it and out POPPED something that looked like ...

Weird fruit ALERT!

 # A WHITE JELLY EYEBALL.

Florence ate one and then spat a shiny black stone into her hand.

"Mmmm, YUMMY. I L♡VE these," she said.

"What are they?" Norman wanted to know.

(Me too.)

"They're DELICIOUS," she said, showing him the contents of her hand.

Yuck

"They're **WEIRD,**" I told her. The whole fruit looked nasty to me. Florence thought it was funny that her FRUIT was causing such a stir. So she peeled two more, popped out the stones and then, along with THREE of MY carrot sticks, she ...

... put them ALL on a plate.

"LOOK!" she said,

LAUGHING!

Ha! Ha!

A kid walking past said,

"EEEWWWWW!

ARE THOSE EYES?"

"NO, silly, they're LYCHEES,"

Florence tried to explain.

But Mark Clump thought she said

LEECHES* and got a bit overexcited.

He stood up and shouted,

"DID YOU KNOW THAT LEECHES

CAN SUCK YOUR BLOOD?"

* Leeches are creatures that look like this. (Bit like a slug.)

I didn't like the sound of LYCHEES  or LEECHES - no one did.

"Y·U·C·K, they look DISGUSTING!" Then Norman thought it would be FUNNY to pick up the plate with the "EYES" on and wave them around so they kind of WOBBLED.

"THEY'RE LOOKING AT YOU!"

Florence was LAUGHING a LOT, which only made him do it some more. He lifted the plate really close to MY face and said,

"EYEBALLS MMMMMMmmmmm."

I PUSHED them away and the LYCHEES
ROLLED off the plate.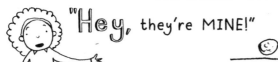

 "Hey, they're MINE!"

Florence tried to grab them but Norman beat
her to it and STUFFED them both

into his mouth.

 "NORMAN!" Florence shouted,

so he spat them back out into his hand.

"I'm NOT going to eat them NOW!"
Florence said crossly.

So he ate them again.

Mmmmm.

"Are they nice?" Solid wondered.

Norman pretended they were the most
DISGUSTING fruit he'd ever eaten in his life.

It was quite convincing until ...

 Uugggg...

... he put his hand to his mouth and said,

"Mmmmm, delicious!"

So we knew he was joking.

We'd been making a lot of noise, so Miss Worthington decided to come over and say,

"Quiet DOWN, or I'll have to SIT here and keep an EYE on you ALL!"

"YES, Mrs Worthington," we said, and we waited until she was gone before Norman made us LAUGH again.

"LOOK! I'm keeping my EYE on you TOO!"

(Florence didn't let him have any more of her LYCHEES.)

That WHOLE **WEIRD** fruit thing took up MOST of our lunchtime, and I can't help thinking that if Florence had brought in an apple instead, NOTHING would have happened.

(UNLESS the apple had a BUG inside, because **THAT'S** happened before.)

HI!

SO... looking through my lunch box today, I am VERY glad there are no nasty surprises inside. (I checked and DOUBLE-checked.)

I eat pretty much everything, apart from the millions of carrot sticks Mum gave me. Not even a RABBIT could eat that many.

(Loads...)

Groan.

(BUT they do make VERY good **VAMPIRE** teeth.)

← See?

Oh ... and there's an ORANGE I haven't eaten yet either.

Sometimes I like to draw pictures around my fruit. I call them FRUIT doodles. As Derek is still eating I get a pen and DRAW around my orange like THIS.

Solid challenged me to do a STRAW doodle ... so here goes.

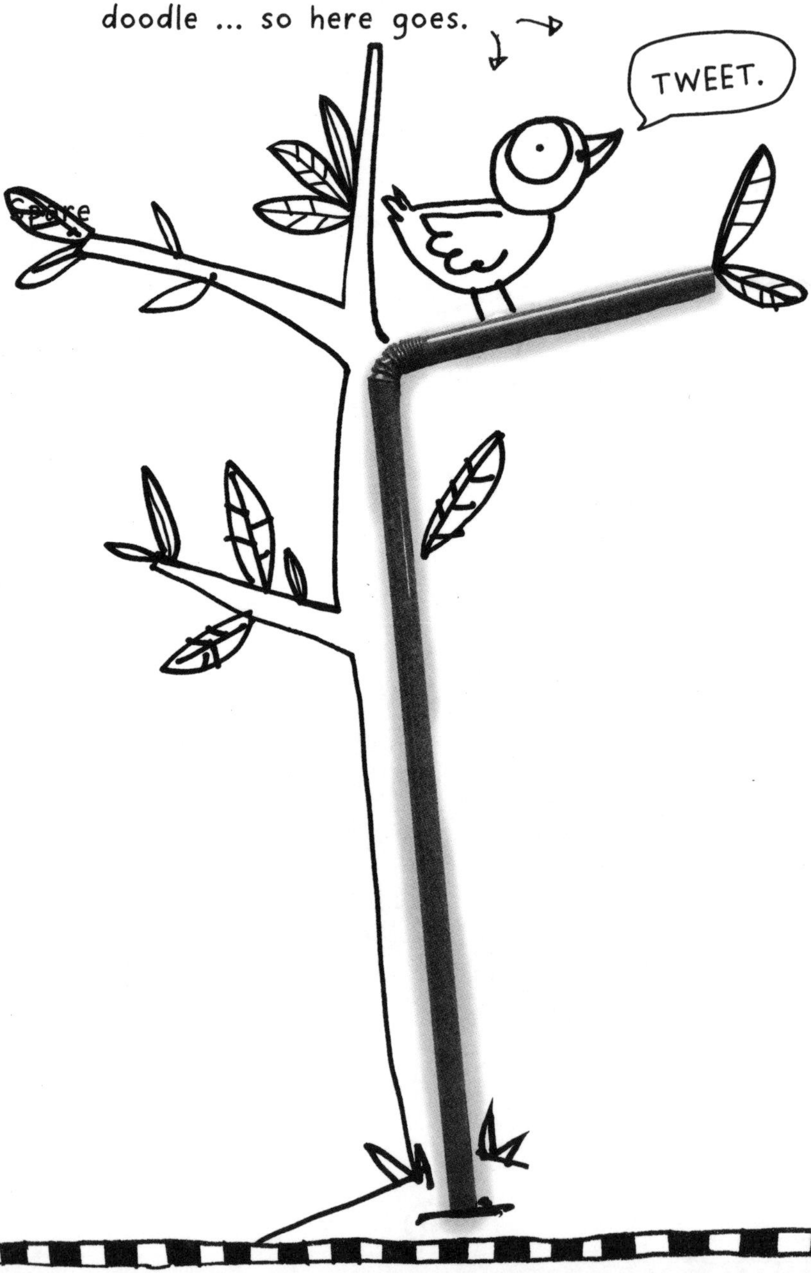

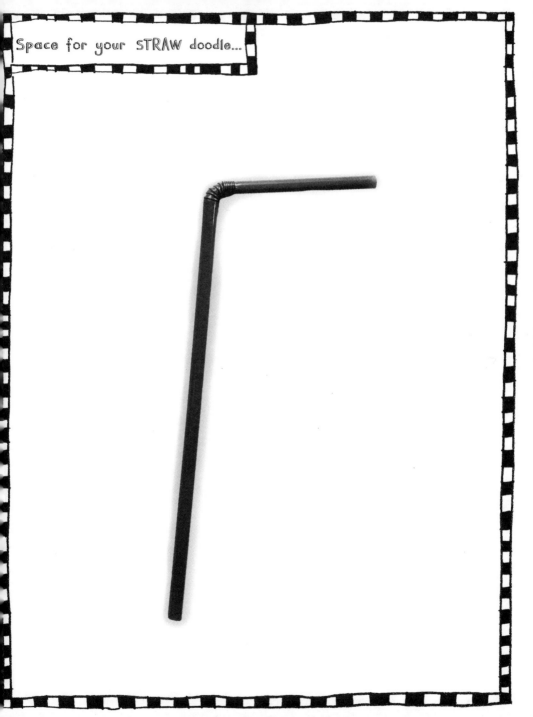

Space for your STRAW doodle...

As well as FRUIT and STRAW doodles,
I like making the peel from my orange into
TEETH like this.

I've still got them in my mouth
when I go back to class. Trying to
answer my name when Mr Fullerman calls the
afternoon register is a bit tricky. I think I've got
away with it until he tells me to **"TAKE OUT
THE ORANGE PEEL TEETH!"**

He's not
impressed

(and still a bit grumpy if you ask me).

Then Brad suddenly puts his hand up and ASKS if
we're going to do anything
FUN for the LAST DAY OF TERM.

"Like we NORMALLY do, sir," he adds.
(GOOD POINT, Brad!)

Mr Fullerman narrows his eyes and says, **"Well, we could have a QUIZ?"**

A *QUIZ?* There's a murmur around the class of "Aaaawwwwwwwwwww" that lets Mr Fullerman know that a QUIZ wasn't exactly what we were all expecting.

"OK. I'll see what I can come up with for tomorrow then."

"Hopefully not just a QUIZ," I whisper to AMY.

"I don't mind a quiz," she tells me.

"That's because you know the answers to the questions. I usually get stuck on a team with YOU KNOW WHO..."

Marcus is listening to me.

"AND THAT SOMEONE always

thinks they know all the answers - but gets

them WRONG."

"You can't be talking about ME because I'm

REALLY GOOD at quizzes," Marcus says.

 "That WOULD be true if you got points for

the WRONG answers."

"Go on then, ASK me a question."

 "Why are you so RUBBISH at quizzes?"

"I'm not - next question."

 "OK - what do you call a BOOMERANG that

doesn't come back?" (Which is a joke that's been

going around school, and a bit like a question.)

"Don't tell me - I KNOW this one," Marcus says ...

while I wait ...

and wait. (He doesn't know it.)

 "The answer is ... A STICK!"

 "I was JUST about to SAY THAT!"

Marcus tells me. (He wasn't.)

"Go on - ASK me another question."

I can't think of another one right now so I just

ask something that's REALLY EASY.

 "What are you doing next week during

the holidays?"

"WHAT kind of question is THAT?"

 "One you should be able to answer."

He thinks I'm trying to trick him.

(I'm not.) I can see he's THINKING about it.

Then he says,

"WELL, now you ask,

I'm going to visit ...

 CHOCOLATE WORLD.

It's supposed to be

FANTASTIC.

AND you'll never believe what they have there."

 "Let me think ... maybe CHOCOLATE?"

I say sarcastically.

"APART from that. They have LOADS of really

amazing *RIDES,* and ONE of them

goes through a RIVER made from ...

GUESS WHAT?"

"Chocolate?"

"WHITE CHOCOLATE,

actually. I can't WAIT!"
Yum

It does sound good, so I ask...

"Hey, Marcus, can you bring me

something NICE back from CHOCOLATE WORLD?"

(I know he won't but it's <u>worth</u> a TRY.)

"WHAT kind of 'something?'"

he asks suspiciously.

"CHOCOLATE would be nice. Just saying!"

"I've got a better idea – I'll get you a badge that says, ⟹ (I didn't go to Chocolate World.) Ha! Ha!

"I'd prefer some chocolate, to be honest."

Marcus is still LAUGHING at his own HILARIOUS joke when the bell goes for the END of school.

Mr Fullerman stands up and starts making announcements about tomorrow.

HE SAYS ⟹

Don't forget that tomorrow is

OK?

SCRAPE

But with everyone SCRAPING their chairs, I can't hear half of it. Oh well — if it was important, we'd have a letter to take home. Besides, I'm in a hurry to LEAVE.

Derek's class often gets out of school before mine. (I don't know WHY!) So he's already waiting outside for me.

Brilliant – LET'S go! he says like he's in a hurry.

Hang on...

I want to have a QUICK CHECK before we start walking. Occasionally, if I'm *lucky,* I'll find the odd 5p or 10p at the bottom of my bag left over from my dinner money. Then we get to STOP at the shop and buy something small to keep us going.

While I'm busy searching, Derek starts to PAT his face.

He's my **BEST** FRIEND and I thought I knew everything about him. But I've NEVER seen him do **that** before.

"WHAT are you doing?" I ask.

Huh?

"**I**'m playing a *tune* on my FACE. You open and close your mouth and it makes a different sort of note. Listen..."

Skills →

Derek demonstrates by playing quite a good version of Happy Birthday on his cheeks. He's in FULL FLOW when I get VERY excited and SHOUT...

FANTASTIC! YEAH!

"Don't go crazy, it's not that good," he says.

"NO — I've found MONEY at the bottom of my bag!"

We celebrate with a HIGH five, and then Derek shows ME how to play a celebratory *tune* as well.

Which is a lot harder than it looks.

We're both in FULL face-patting FLOW when AMY and her friends walk past.

"Band practice started already then?" she LAUGHS.

It's a good time to stop anyway.

"Your face is red,"

Derek tells me.

"So is yours,"

I say.

We leave a good GAP between AMY and the

other girls before setting off for home.

The FIRST thing I do when I get home is finish eating the  FRUIT CHEW I bought so Mum doesn't know I've been to the shop. (Done.) She's been getting everything sorted for our holiday, and straight away she says ...

Let's get your bag PACKED, TOM.

"What, now? We're not leaving yet. I can do my own packing,"

I tell Mum confidently.

"I know you CAN, but remember the last time you packed and you forgot to bring any PANTS?"

She had to remind me

about THAT.

"Some things are essential."

"It's OK, Mum, I'll bring my PANTS!"

I say quickly so she doesn't KEEP on talking about them.

"I meant THESE plastic containers - they're always useful on holiday," Mum tells me.

(Really? I don't know why - but at least she didn't say PANTS again.)

"Leave out what you want to take and I'll pack it for you. INCLUDING some clean PANTS."

(Groan...)

We're going on HOLIDAY to a place called:

PINE TREE RIVIERA

I've seen pictures and it looks a lot fancier than the campsites we normally go to.

Dad says we're staying in a  mobile villa, which sounds better than a TENT.

The only BAD thing about the holiday is ...

Delia is coming too.

She's not exactly over the moon about it either.

The other day in the kitchen, Mum and Dad had a BIG "discussion" about WHY Delia couldn't stay at home. I wasn't supposed to hear but it was HARD not to, especially when Delia shouted,

"But I don't even LIKE holidays OR the SUN."

Dad said she didn't have to worry about the SUN as it would probably rain every day anyway.

"That's another reason NOT to come then," Delia told them.

Mum said it wasn't going to rain. "Well, not *EVERY* day. Come on, Delia – being together for a *lovely* family holiday will be *FUN*!"

"FUN is the one thing it WON'T be," Delia told them. I could tell she wasn't happy. She was grumbling about lots of things and kept saying, "MY friends are doing THIS..." and "My friends are doing THAT..."

I had to hand it to her, she was really trying her best NOT to come away with us.

If it was up to ME that chat would have gone more like THIS:

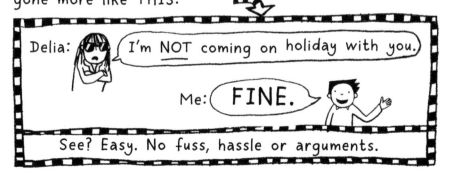

Delia: I'm NOT coming on holiday with you.

Me: FINE.

See? Easy. No fuss, hassle or arguments.

I stood outside and pressed my EAR against the door to HEAR more of the conversation, but it started to get a bit MUFFLED. So in the end I just pretended I didn't know it was a PRIVATE chat and walked in. Dad was in the middle of saying,

"IF we agree, you'll have to share a room."

And that's when I PANICKED.
SHARE A ROOM WITH DELIA? NO WAY!

"I'm NOT SHARING A ROOM!"

I shouted.

"**Y**OU don't have to SHARE a room, Tom. We're talking to Delia. Out you go."

I was SO **relieved** that I didn't really think any more about it.

I just went and did some drawing and looked forward to the holiday instead.

LAST DAY OF SCHOOL.

YEAH!

It's amazing the difference one day can make. This morning I've woken up EXTRA early 👀 and decided that I'm going to call on Derek for a change. Normally he ends up waiting for me.

I get all my stuff together for school, which doesn't take long. Then I have a SWIFT breakfast before I head over to Derek's.

Toast

I ring the doorbell quite a few times before someone comes to open it.

It's Derek's dad - and from the way he looks I'm guessing he's only just woken up.

"TOM! You're early - Derek's not ready yet. Come in and wait for him."

Rooster is VERY excited to see me.

Mr Fingle says,
"Down, Rooster!"

(Too late.)

"Leave Tom alone," he adds while taking me into

the kitchen. (Rooster follows.)

"Help yourself to some breakfast — I'll
get Derek to hurry up." Then he tells

Rooster to "STAY!" but that doesn't work either.

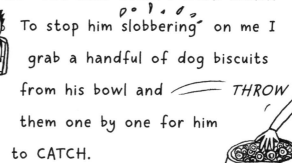

To stop him slobbering on me I

grab a handful of dog biscuits

from his bowl and   *THROW*

them one by one for him

to CATCH.

Rooster

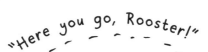

"Here you go, Rooster!"

He's better at

catching them ...

... than I am at throwing them.

Some land in a bowl of cereal.

I'm about to try and take them

out when Derek and **Mr Fingle** come in.

So I put the spoon down quickly.

"Did you want some breakfast, Tom?"

Mr Fingle asks me.

"Errrrr... No, thanks. I've eaten already."

"I'll have these then, unless you want them, Derek?"

"I'll pour my own bowl," he says, and I breathe

a sigh of relief. Then **Mr Fingle** sits down and

starts EATING the DOG TREATS!

"It's not too late to change your mind?"

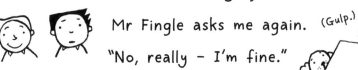 Mr Fingle asks me again. (Gulp.)

"No, really – I'm fine."

I keep quiet as Derek and his dad eat breakfast.

SILENCE

"You're EARLY," Derek says and I just nod.

"I'm sure we're supposed to be doing SOMETHING special TODAY, but I can't remember WHAT," he adds, looking at me.

"It's the last day of term if that's what you mean?"

Then Rooster starts crunching his dog biscuits really loudly in the corner and Mr Fingle pulls a FACE.

Crunch
Crunch
Crunch
Crunch

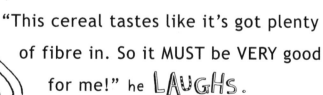

"This cereal tastes like it's got plenty of fibre in. So it MUST be VERY good for me!" he LAUGHS.

(I don't say a word.)

Dog treat

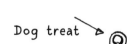

Derek and I are walking to school when I ask him ...

"Have you ever eaten one of Rooster's dog biscuits?"

"No — why?"

"Because I think your dad just has."

Luckily, when I tell Derek what happened he thinks it's HILARIOUS.

"So if I throw a BALL for Rooster and Dad JUMPS UP to catch it, now I'll know WHY!"

he chuckles.

Woof!

(Fetch!)

83

We're nearly at the school gates and Derek
is STILL convinced that SOMETHING
is happening...

"It's the last day of term. If we've forgotten
something, how bad can it be?"

"...QUITE bad," Derek says.

It's No School Uniform Day.

"Awwww - the ONE time we could wear what we want, and LOOK at us BOTH."

 "I knew I'd forgotten something."

Looking around I try to be **POSITIVE** and tell Derek ...

"Don't PANIC - I'm sure we won't be the ONLY kids wearing our uniform. You'll see."

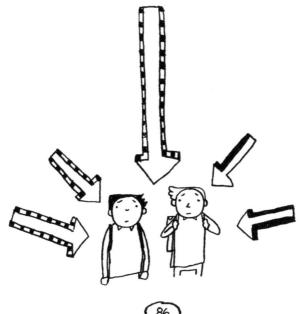

"We could go home and change?" I suggest.

Derek points at Mr Keen

who's standing by the school gates.

"It's too late – he wouldn't let us leave NOW."

(True.)

I think about taking off my sweatshirt or rolling up

the sleeves to make my uniform LOOK different.

There must be SOMETHING

I can do...

Think...   Think...   ?

THEN

✩ PING! ✩ ✩

I HAVE A

PLAN!

"I KNOW what to do!"  I tell Derek.
FIRST I need a PEN.

SO I take one out of my bag.

"You're going to draw me a picture?" he wonders.

"SORT OF. You know we have white T-shirts in our PE bags?"

 "The ones hanging up in the cloakroom
IN SCHOOL?"

 "THAT'S RIGHT! How about I DRAW a
DOGZOMBIES BAND LOGO on them?"

"BRILLIANT! But when are you going to do
THAT?" Derek asks.

 It's a good point. We're not allowed into
school YET.

Hmmmmmm...

I'm just wondering what to do next when WHO should open the door right in front of us?

ONLY ⇨ **Buster Jones.**

(He's behaving himself these days and even being helpful by putting out chairs for assembly.)

 "BUSTER! KEEP THAT DOOR OPEN! PLEASE," I shout.

"Sorry, Gatesy, you're not allowed. I'll get into trouble if I let you inside...

What's with the UNIFORM?"

"We forgot it was No Uniform Day. IF you let us in we can get our PE T-shirts from the cloakroom and wear those instead." Hmmmmmmm...

Buster doesn't look convinced.

"It won't take long - I have

SUPER good NINJA SKILLS!

Buster narrows his eyes and thinks for a while, and eventually says, "OK, but not BOTH of you - just Tom. AND don't tell ANYONE I let you in or you'll be in trouble with ME." GULP...

"Thanks, Buster." I take a deep breath and step silently into school, ready to put my skills into action.

I check left and right, then sneak along the wall.

So far so good...

I edge closer ...

and closer ...

until **YES!**

I've MADE IT!

Our PE bags are easy to find so I $=$ **GRAB** them and CREEP back towards the door. Buster and Derek are WAVING furiously at me to ↱

HURRY UP!

I'm nearly there when ...

Mrs Worthington suddenly **APPEARS!**

So I hide and stay VERY still.

"It's nice to see you BOYS are KEEN to come into school, but you're a bit early. Now close the door behind you, please."

I can see Derek trying to say something.

 "But... Errrrr..."

It's no good. Mrs Worthington closes the door and I'm left inside – hiding. As she walks away, I decide to make a =====*DASH* for freedom.

 Then Mr Sprocket walks past and I'm forced to stay `HIDDEN` until the bell goes for the start of school.

Ding! Ding! Ding! I make my way to class and pretend I'm just **VERY** early (which is unusual for me).

Mr Fullerman thinks so, too.

"Is THAT really YOU, Tom?"

 Yes, sir. I'm KEEN...

But then I remember that Derek has my bag and I'm still in my uniform. So I SAY ...

 "I'm **KEEN** to change OUT of my uniform and into my T-shirt. After I've drawn on it. That's why I'm EARLY."

Mr Fullerman sighs.

"Go on then, HURRY up."

(Mr Fullerman is in a better mood than yesterday, so I borrow some pens and start doodling.)

93  Thanks, sir.

Me doodling on my T-shirt

If I do say so MYSELF, they look **ACE.**

Just as Derek appears with my bag I finish his T-shirt. We do a SUPER-SPEEDY SWAP and I breathe a sigh of RELIEF THAT:

1. I didn't get caught by Mrs. Worthingtash.
2. We are no longer the school uniform NERDS.

That badge of honour goes to Marcus Meldrew, who didn't realize it was <u>NO</u> Uniform Day either. (Shame.)

"I FORGOT," Marcus says, looking REALLY fed up.

It's bad enough sitting next to him when he's in a

GOOD mood (and being all SMUG).

But when he's in a BAD mood it's even WORSE.

As it's the LAST day of term and I'm feeling

generous, I show Marcus my T-shirt.

"I COULD do one for you, IF you like?"

Marcus looks at me suspiciously.

"What do you want?"

"Nothing – just don't be miserable ALL day."

"I'll get my PE T-shirt then. But I don't

want YOUR band name on the front.

Just my name, OK!" he says, cheering up a bit.

 "Fine, but you'd better hurry up. We don't have much time."

Mr Fullerman is arranging some stuff on a table as the other kids arrive for class. While he's still busy, Marcus gets me his T-shirt and I start drawing on it as he WATCHES. A bit too closely for my liking.

"Don't spell my name wrong," he tells me. (I wasn't going to, but now he's said that it's VERY tempting to write

MORCUS NORCUS MERCUS MARKUS PARCUS

... but I don't.)

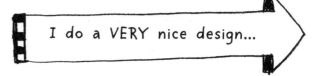 I do a VERY nice design...

This is the one I did for Marcus.

On the FRONT

Here's a spare T-shirt to draw on.

Here's <u>MY</u> DESIGN

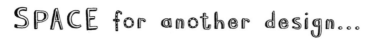

SPACE for another design...

I finish what I think is a very good doodle on Marcus's T-shirt when he says, "What's going on the BACK? It's a bit EMPTY."

EMPTY

"Nothing. I was just helping you out, remember?"

"Can you do something else? NOT your band logo," Marcus says, IGNORING what I just said.

"Pass it here *quickly* - I'll draw one of my monsters," I SIGH.

I do **this** and Marcus puts it on. He even says, "Thanks," which is something.

Then he starts grumbling AGAIN!

"It still feels a bit like school uniform," he moans.

"You don't HAVE to wear it," I point out.

"I suppose it's better than **NOTHING.**"

I've had enough of him complaining so I decide to do something about it.

"Hey, Marcus – the monster needs finishing off PROPERLY. That might help."

"I'm NOT taking my T-shirt off," he tells me.

"You don't have to — just turn round and try to keep STILL."

"Don't draw anything stupid!" Marcus says.

"AS IF..."
But now he's said THAT...

It's too good an opportunity to MISS.

There ... all done.

(I think it's an improvement.)

Mr Fullerman is looking much HAPPIER* today.

It's like we've got a different teacher.

"Hello, Class 5F! Who's pleased it's the
LAST DAY OF TERM?"

(I think Mr Fullerman is.)

I shout ME! along with the rest

of the class.

"And who's ready for our FANTASTIC
end-of-term TRUE or FALSE Quiz?"

 he adds excitedly.

True or False - see how well you can do...

		TRUE	FALS
1	A penguin can't fly, so it's NOT a bird.		
2	A pineapple grows on a tree.		
3	A spider has EIGHT legs.		
4	If you mix yellow and blue, you get purple.		
5	Unicorns really exist.		
6	Sydney is the capital of Australia.		
7	Honey is made by bees.		
8	Dodos really did exist.		
9	If you mix yellow and red, you get orange.		
10	The fastest animal on land is the leopard.		

Sort of...

(I suppose it's better than maths.)

Mr Fullerman divides us all into TWO Big TEAMS.

AMY'S lucky – she's been moved to sit with Indrani. I end up working with – GUESS WHO?

MARCUS ➡ (Great.)

"Don't mess up the answers will you?" he says as we get passed a quiz sheet.

"It's TRUE or FALSE – the answers are on the paper. We just have to pick the right one. HOW hard can it be?"

"Easy for ME. I'm good at quizzes, remember?"

(We'll see about that...)

And here are some I made up.

	TRUE	FALSE
Marcus has a really BIG dog as a pet.		
Mrs Worthington has a beard.		
DUDE3 are the best band in the world.		
Caramel wafers are delicious.		
The cousins hate scary films.		
Uncle Kevin knows everything.		
Mr Fullerman's eyes are as BIG as PLATES.		
School photos are never a good experience.		
Delia is not always grumpy.		
Me and Derek have always been best friends.		

ANSWERS ON PAGE 243

The QUIZ was more FUN than I thought.
We got MOST of the questions RIGHT, although
I got ONE wrong and now Marcus won't stop
going ON about it.
He turns round and asks anyone
who'll listen...

HEY! WHO thinks that
UNICORNS really EXIST?
NO ONE...?
It's just you
then, TOM.

"I got confused!" I explain. I'm tempted to
tell him what's written on the back of his
T-shirt, but I don't. Besides, my ONE
wrong answer doesn't stop our team from winning.
Which is something.

AND because our team WON, Mr Fullerman says we get FIRST pick of the RAFFLE TICKETS. He's set up a WHOLE table of PRIZES – which is VERY unexpected and a nice end-of-term SURPRISE. ☺

END-OF-TERM RAFFLE

"No one will miss out. There's SOMETHING for ALL of you," he assures us. The first chance I get to wander casually past the table and CHECK OUT what's up for grabs – I DO.

Mark Clump and I are discussing what we'd like to WIN when Leroy points out, "It looks like Mr Fullerman's cleared out all his office stuff. No sweets or anything."

(He's not wrong.)

Marcus has been LOOKING at the prizes as well. "I want that PACK of PENS and DEFINITELY NOT that MASSIVE pack of STICKY notes. What kind of a prize is THAT?"

"You don't get to choose — it's just LUCK," AMY tells Marcus. Then she looks at his T-shirt and says, "Nice drawing. Did you do it, Tom?"

"Do you like it?" I ask, but Marcus BUTTS in and says, "He's better at drawing than he is at QUIZZES — AREN'T you?"

"You should check out the monster I did on the BACK of his T-shirt," I tell AMY. "That's pretty good too."

HELPFULLY, Marcus actually TURNS round to show her.

That's even better.

Shhh.

Then Mr Fullerman begins to pick out NUMBERS for the RAFFLE — so we keep quiet and LISTEN.

When Marcus hears his number (Yes!) called he's VERY HAPPY to find his prize is a

fancy notebook and PEN.

AMY gets a pair of SOCKS and when my

NUMBER **3** gets called out, I RUSH up and

SPOT that 3 is STUCK ON ⟹

I'm REALLY HAPPY with my prize, but Marcus thinks it's a DISASTER.

"HA! I'm glad I didn't win those sticky notes. That's the WORST prize EVER!"

"Well I don't think so - STICKY NOTES are really useful for all kinds of things."

"LIKE WHAT?" Marcus scoffs.

"You can play the STICKY NOTE GAME, where you write something on a NOTE then stick it on the other person's head - LIKE THIS - and you have to GUESS what or who you are," I explain.

"BIG DEAL - I prefer my notebook and pen. Sticky notes are a bit RUBBISH, you have to admit."

Marcus is WRONG about sticky NOTES - there are SO MANY things you can do with them ... ➡

Apart from putting notes on Marcus's back I'm already finding a TON of other things to do with the sticky notes.

What else to draw? Hmmmmmm....

My monster

Finish the doodle, then draw your own.

I'm STILL {thinking} 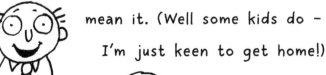 of other things to do with my sticky notes when the (bell) FINALLY goes for the end of school. Mr Fullerman tell us to ...

Have a WONDERFUL HOLIDAY and see you in a week. Don't forget to FINISH off ALL your work as time will FLY by. So get EVERYTHING done, OK, Class 5F?

We say, "YES, SIR!" like we really mean it. (Well some kids do – I'm just keen to get home!)

This holiday is going to be the BEST EVER.

I'm really looking forward to going away.
I don't even mind when Marcus BARGES past me
because it's a LOT of ☆FUN☆ watching him SHARE
my sticky note messages with everyone as he walks
through the school.

(So useful.)

Here are a few messages I'm taking on holiday with me.

I've got ONE

BRAIN

CELL.

(And here it is...)

This one's for Delia.

This one's to protect my SNACKS.

(Also true.) →

WARNING:

I HAVE licked this BISCUIT.

(Eat it if you DARE.)

Any other
ideas for
stickers

As I pass Dad my bag I notice that the EXTRA seat is set up right at the back of the car.

Which makes me WONDER...

What's going on?

THAT seat only gets put up if we're giving other people a RIDE. (I'm usually the one who ends up sitting in it.)

 Which is the {FIRST} bit of the surprise.

Then Dad says to me,

Tom, you're in the BACK.

"Why do I have to SIT there? Can't I sit where I normally do?"

"You have to sit in the back because we're picking up Avril on the way."

"AVRIL! WHY - WHAT FOR?"

Shocked face

Most of the time I like {surprises.} I've already seen pictures of where we are staying on holiday. So _THAT_ isn't going to be a surprise. It looks like a nice place, all surrounded by PINE TREES and not far from the beach.

I am very EXCITED!

With my bag all packed (by Mum in the end), I go outside so Dad can squash it into the car.

He is doing his best to fit EVERYTHING in, but it isn't going to be easy.

"WHO needs THIS many plastic CONTAINERS?" he asks me as TWO fall out of the picnic bag. "Your Mum's OBSESSED with them!"

(I heard that!) Mum grumbles from the house. She can hear everything (she has BAT ears).

D ad doesn't answer me straight away so I say, "She's NOT coming on holiday with us, is she?"

He mutters something about Delia wanting a friend with her and how they don't have much CHOICE if they want Delia to come.

 "SO LEAVE Delia behind!" I suggest.

This is a BIG SURPRISE

and NOT one I was expecting.
(Definitely NOT one I am happy about.)

Delia and **Avril** have been friends for a while and, apart from the fact that **Avril** is a lot shorter than Delia, they look quite similar in a **gloomy** kind of way. At least **Avril** doesn't

`TALK` very much, so she won't be too chatty in the car. THAT'S SOMETHING.

Mum always tries really hard to make conversation with **Avril** But she only ever says things like:

 Yes

 No...

 Kind of...

 Not really

And that's about it.
Avril coming with us is NOT my idea of a

 SURPRISE.

I'm still getting over this NEWS when Mum
comes out to the car and says,
"I'm sorry, Tom – didn't we tell you
Avril was coming with us?"

"NO! Why does Delia get to bring
a friend and I DON'T?" I ask.

"There's not enough room. Maybe NEXT time
YOU can bring someone," Mum tells me –
which is now LOGGED in my BRAIN and WILL be
remembered and brought
up again the next Holiday. Derek.
time we go away.

"It was ALSO the ONLY way we could
get Delia not to spend the whole time sulking.
You know what she's like sometimes – TEENAGERS
and all that," Mum adds like it's an

EXCUSE.

"Why does **Avril** have to come with us?" I ask Dad again. It doesn't seem fair to me.

"Because we couldn't leave Delia at home on her **OWN** so we agreed she could bring a friend. At least NOW she won't spend the **WHOLE** time being GRUMPY!"

"She's always grumpy," I point out. Then Mum comes out holding more bags and tells me, "Delia and **Avril** will hang out together, and _you_ get to hang out with **US!**"

"Think of the ☆**FUN**☆ things we're going to be able to do together!" Dad says enthusiastically.

"What kind of things?" I ask, because I'm NOT convinced that Delia and **Avril** aren't going to spoil my **WHOLE** holiday.

Dad says we'll be ... swimming, fishing, rock pooling, boogie boarding, EVEN AND surfing.

When Dad says "surfing", Mum makes a
BIG SCOFF noise.
 "You're going SURFING, Frank. REALLY?"

"What do you mean? I'm a natural
– you'll see," Dad says while doing
a SURF action.

 "All I can SEE is ... SURFING
in the morning, then HOSPITAL in the
afternoon," Mum says, LAUGHING.

"You might be SURPRISED," Dad tells her.

(I'm STILL SURPRISED that **Avril** is
coming on holiday with us ... GROAN!)

Mum and Dad carry on packing the car and I SQUEEZE into my BACK SEAT and TRY to get comfortable. Delia turns up when everything's done. (TYPICAL.)

 She SLUMPS down ... and doesn't say a WORD. So I don't either.

(NOT YET anyway.)

We're almost ready to go when Dad wants to DOUBLE-check that all the PLUGS are OFF.

Good idea, Mum agrees, and they both go back to the house.

Delia SIGHS , while I get my snacks ready for the journey.

—Special snack tin

It's not too long before they're back and Mum's clutching another plastic container.

"Glad I didn't forget THIS," she says, SQUEEZING it into a tiny space by her feet.

"That is SUCH a relief," Dad tells her.

"All right, Frank ... shall we go? Have you got everything?" Mum asks us.

"There's NO room for anything ELSE," Delia says.

"Like Avril," I mutter, and Mum gives me a LOOK.

"Have you been to the bathroom. Do you have a TISSUE for your nose?" she wants to know.

I say "YES!" to both questions because I'm FINE.

Then OFF we go.

We've only just driven round the corner ...

... when I do my first SNIFF.

I didn't even know I was sniffing, but by the THIRD time Delia says I'm (GROSS, Mum passes me a whole WODGE of tissues.

"DON'T SNIFF!"

she tells me.

(It's hard NOT to now.)

Sniff
Sniff
Sniff

Sniff
Sniff

I eventually stop sniffing...

Avril doesn't live far away, and as we pull up to her house, Mum starts to get out of the car.

"Where are YOU going?"
Delia wants to know.

"I'm going to say a quick hello to Avril's mum."

"WHY? We're not KIDS!" Delia's not happy, but it's too late because Avril and her mum are already walking towards the car.

Avril looks like Delia (grumpy), and NOT that excited to be coming with us. BUT Avril's mum can't stop SMILING and WAVING.

"It's so NICE of you to bring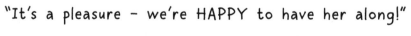
Avril on holiday!" she tells Mum.

"It's a pleasure – we're HAPPY to have her along!"

(I'm NOT.)

As we drive off **Avril's** mum is still WAVING and shouting.

BYE! Bye-bye! Take care! Bye-bye!

(Avril says nothing.)

 Dad tells **Avril** it's lovely to have her with us.

"Are we all looking forward to doing LOTS of HIKING and climbing up mountains then?"

 "Don't worry — he's joking. See what I have to put up with?" Delia says to **Avril**.

Then she gets out her laptop and they both plug in their headphones and put on a film. I can just about SEE what they're watching. BUT I can't HEAR it. So I *LEAN* in for a closer look. Bit closer... CLOSER... Until Delia notices and moves the whole screen so I can't see a thing.

"Don't be annoying, Tom," she tells me.

Oh well. I have PLENTY of other things I can do. Like sort out my SNACKS,  have my juice (I drink BOTH of them), and get out my sticky notes and DECIDE what to write on the next one (which takes me a while). I finally decide on THIS. ☆

All I have to do now is work out HOW to sneak it on to her BACK.

(Mission accomplished.)

We've driven past a few service stations already when Mum asks ...

Does ANYONE need to use the bathroom?

NO ONE does.

Well, I do a BIT, but I'm OK for NOW. So I don't say anything.

About ten minutes later I realize that I'm DESPERATE!

"Can we STOP soon?" I ask, slightly urgently.

"Why didn't you say something EARLIER?" Dad says.

"You'll have to HOLD on until we pass ANOTHER service station. It shouldn't be TOO LONG," Mum assures me.

(I hope not.)

TWENTY MINUTES LATER - WE'RE STILL
DRIVING! ))) (I'm wriggling around a lot.)
Delia decides that RIGHT NOW is a perfect time to
open her [WATER] bottle and have a drink.

 Glug
Glug
Glug

She starts *SWISHING* the
water around so I can HEAR it.

"Does anyone else want some **WATER**?"
(Delia knows EXACTLY what she's doing.)

SLOSH *Swish* SLOSH )))

"TELL DELIA TO STOP,"

I say, panicking a bit.

"How long before we're there?"

Delia carries on saying, "Can't I have
a NICE COOL drink of WATER?"

Dad can HEAR the desperation in my voice and
manages to find a garage. We pull over
and I **DASH** to the bathroom.

[Before] ➡

AFTER

(Which is a RELIEF.)

Happy face

LEAP!

Things get EVEN better when I see Delia walking around with my sticky note message still on her back...

UNTIL Avril spots it and takes it off.

Awww.

As I get back to the car Delia is SHOWING my note to Mum and Dad, and she tells me CROSSLY,

"NO MORE STICKY NOTES ...

OR ELSE!"

141

Which is basically an
OFFICIAL challenge for
me to do it AGAIN.

(RESULT!)

Car journeys always make me feel sleepy. So now
seems like a good time to have a NAP.

 zzzzzzz   I'm dozing off when I hear Delia
whispering about ME to Avril.
(I keep listening with my eyes closed.)

She says, "When he's asleep is the only
time he's NOT annoying. If he starts to **BUG**
you, just IGNORE him and EVENTUALLY he'll go
AWAY."

She's talking about ME like I'm some kind
of :RASH. So I decide to SAY the
THREE WORDS that no one wants to hear on a car
journey...

"I FEEL CARSICK..."

Ewww.

Then I sit back and watch Delia panic.

Avril moves away from me as far as she can.

"For goodness' sake, pass this to Tom - quickly!"

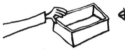 ← (It's one of those plastic containers.)

RELUCTANTLY, Delia does.

"And don't EAT any more SNACKS," she adds.

Thanks to my **SUPER GOOD** acting **SKILLS**,

Delia and **Avril** keep lurching away from

me EVERY TIME I

COUGH! or  **GROAN...**

I manage to keep it up for quite a while.

It's very entertaining ... FOR ME.

Mum suggests we should play a game of
👁 **I SPY**. "It might take your mind OFF

feeling carsick," she adds.

 "**OK**," I say in a slightly weak voice.

I'm allowed to go first.

(Not surprisingly, Delia and **Avril** don't join in.)

"I SPY with my little **EYE** something beginning

with **C**."

Cake?
Cows? Cars?
Chocolate? Caterpillar?
Cups? Clouds? Coffee?
Crayon? Cat? Camel?

Dad's being silly now, so I ask if they need a clue.

"This **C** could be everywhere soon."

"Go on, tell us."

I do a little cough ... and then say, "**C**ARSICK,"

and wave around the plastic box, which makes Delia

and **Avril** move away.

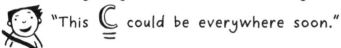

Gross...

Ha! Ha!

We stop playing I SPY because Dad wants to keep a LOOK OUT for signs to the VILLA.

"Is it my imagination or is the SKY getting **DARKER** and STORMIER?" Mum says, looking UP.

"It's your imagination – there's SUN over there," Dad says cheerily.

"But we're not driving that way," I point out.

"EXACTLY," Mum agrees.

"Glad you're feeling better, Tom," Dad says to me.

Sun ↓   Cloud ↓

Then he SPOTS the FIRST SIGN and changes the subject.

LOOK! There IT IS! ➡

PINE TREE RIVIERA 🌲

Mum and I do a **CHEER!** Delia mutters,

"At last." (Avril keeps quiet.) Dad follows more

signs and keeps driving.

"There are a LOT of PINE TREES

around here, aren't there?" I say,

looking out of the window.

"He's a child genius," Delia mutters.

"Everyone can THANK ME for not getting

LOST once," Dad tells us.

"You've done a GREAT JOB," Mum agrees.

"I can't wait to see the villa!" I say.

Dad stops the car at what he thinks is the right place.

"I followed the SIGNS - this must be it."

"Are you SURE?" Mum says, because it doesn't look much like the pictures.

"It looks like a DUMP," Delia grumbles. Avril just STARES like she's in a TRANCE, which I think is WEIRD.

"Let's go inside - I'm sure it'll be LOVELY once we get settled," Dad says, trying to make us all feel better.

"I hope so," Mum sighs.
We gather up all the bags and make our way to the "mobile villa".

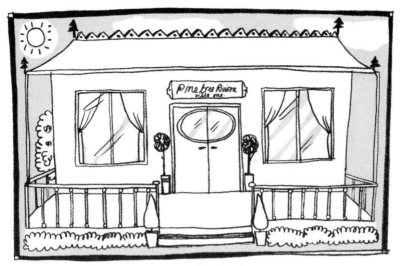

Here's what it looked like in the brochure.

Here's what it looks like in REAL LIFE.

At least it isn't a TENT. AND I get to have my own room.

We're away and having a nice break. How bad could it be?

THEN IT STARTED TO
RAIN...

... and it didn't STOP RAINING for almost the
WHOLE ENTIRE HOLIDAY.

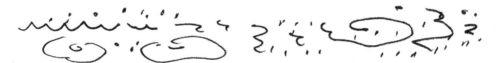

This was SUPPOSED to be the start of a FUN-
PACKED few days. I tried to keep myself busy.
In the end I kept a HOLIDAY DIARY.

Very damp sticky note

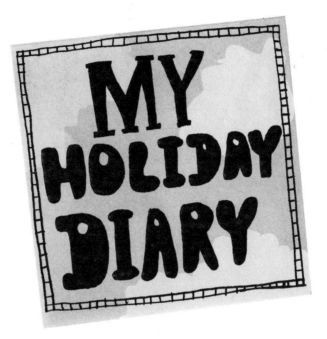

(Enjoy...) ⟹

← Wet paper

Pen - ready to go...

MY
DIARY

FULL
OF
IMPORTANT
STUFF ➡

Damp patch

DATE	DAY ONE	
Mood	Damp	**My Plans for the Day**
Weather	Damp	Have a nice time.

Dear Diary,

(That's what you're supposed to say apparently.)
I'm on holiday and so far things aren't going
too well. On the HOLIDAY METER, it's hovering
around the "bit RUBBISH" end.

There are LOTS of reasons for this, but
MOSTLY it is because of ...

Drum roll...

RAIN, wind,

MORE RAIN AND more wind,

Delia moaning,  "Moan Moan" Avril (just being here),

MUM ⇨ <u>NOT</u> packing LOADS of the stuff that I left out to BRING! 😖

Today is the <u>FIRST DAY</u> staying at the PINE TREE RIVIERA. Normally I wouldn't be writing ANYTHING on my holiday (unless Mum and Dad were FORCING me to write POSTCARDS – which might still happen). But Mum gave me this  a few weeks ago and told me it might be FUN to do while we're away. I said, "Hmmmmmm, MAYBE."

(Which is CODE for ...

NO WAY - YOU HAVE TO BE

 KIDDING!)

Because WHO wants to write a DIARY on holiday?

NOT ME – that's for sure. I was going to be FAR too BUSY enjoying myself and doing LOADS of other interesting things.

OR THAT'S what I THOUGHT.

Mum brought it with her anyway, so here I am *writing* away and (SHOCK HORROR) I'm actually enjoying it. I could have filled up the whole BOOK already.

Ha! Ha!

AT FIRST Mum and Dad were PLEASED to see me keeping a RECORD of EVERYTHING that's happening. But then things started to go WRONG.

"Will your teachers see this?" Mum wondered. I said, "No," but that didn't STOP me from feeling like I was a REPORTER on a NEWSPAPER telling all the LATEST STORIES. (So many.)

PINE TREE NEWS

RAIN

RUINS FAMILY HOLIDAY

Favourite son Tom Gates with his diary

Mr & Mrs Gates were SHOCKED that their villa at the Pine Tree Riviera was SUCH a WRECK. "I feel like a fool for coming here," Mr Gates said.

"The roof leaks — and the rain hasn't helped," Mrs Gates said.

Their son Tom has been keeping a DIARY of the WHOLE EVENT. Tom is very SMART.

Make up your OWN news story here:

PINE TREE NEWS

Some of my diary pages are a bit soggy and damp. (That happened when we drove up to the "VILLA".)

Dad kept saying "THIS CAN'T be the place I booked - it looks NOTHING like the PHOTO."

Silence

Mum looked ~~a bit~~ VERY surprised. She could hardly speak.

Delia and Avril didn't say much either.

"I'm SURE it's MUCH NICER inside," Dad told us.

"I hope so," Mum sighed, putting her handbag on her head and making a DASH through the rain as we followed. (Delia and Avril stayed in the car.) She took out the key but couldn't seem to get the door open. She wiggled it around as we got soaking wet.

My diary

Dad had a go but he couldn't
open it either.
Then he spotted a small window
and LOOKED at ME
like he had an idea.

"Tom could open the door from the inside,"
he said, POINTING at the open window.
Mum wasn't sure it was such a good idea, so I
reminded them I have "SUPER GOOD NINJA
jumping and landing SKILLS. I'll be OK."

Mum said, "IS IT SAFE?"
Delia shouted from the car,
WHO CARES? Just let him do it! PLEASE...
So Dad lifted me up and I climbed in slowly
(which was pretty easy).
I opened the door and for a very
short time - EVERYONE WAS HAPPY...

 **But that** didn't last **LONG...** Dad thought

the "villa" looked just as shabby on the inside

as it was on the outside.

 "I can't believe we

came ALL THAT WAY JUST TO BE HERE,"

 Delia said, being her usual helpful self.

Avril kept quiet.

I didn't think it was *THAT* bad.

"Why don't you all take your bags and go and

find your rooms," Mum said, trying to be positive.

Which seemed like a good idea. Delia and **Avril**

disappeared quickly and NABBED what turned

out to be the **BEST** room in the "villa".

"You're over there," she told me, pointing to

something that looked like a cupboard.

The door was VERY small and when I opened it, so was the space inside.

But I didn't mind. At least I wasn't sharing. I could hear Mum and Dad outside talking as they realized Delia and Avril were in THEIR room.

"If we ask them to move NOW Delia will be GRUMPY the WHOLE holiday. Is it worth it?"

"I suppose NOT. Let's have an argument-FREE holiday, shall we?"

"Live in HOPE," Dad sighed.

"You can HAVE MY ROOM!" I shouted.

Mum looked in and said it was "really cosy" and perfect for me.

(I'm guessing "COSY" means tiny.)

"We're going to have a GREAT time, I promise," she added, giving me a hug and then BASHING her head on the ceiling.

Mum often says ONE thing but means something else. Here are some of HER FAVOURITE SAYINGS:

Mum SAYS	Mum MEANS
I'll THINK about it.	No chance.
No more TV – it's time for bed.	I want to watch MY programmes now.
That looks interesting.	I don't know what you're doing.
Finish your vegetables.	No pudding unless you finish your vegetables.
Uncle Kevin's coming round.	OH NO! Uncle Kevin's coming round.

Here is some SPACE for another LIST:

_ _ _ _ _ _ _ _ _ _ SAYS | _ _ _ _ _ _ _ _ _ MEANS

Dear Diary, ☆ ☆ ☆

(It's night-time in case you're wondering WHY
my writing's a bit wobbly.)
I'm doing this with a TORCH
under my bedcovers. I can't
turn on a light because the electricity went
OFF when Dad was trying to make some dinner.
We all went to bed early after that happened –
with a sandwich.

Right now DELIA has WOKEN me up
and I can hear her COMPLAINING to Mum
and Dad ... about Avril.

 She's telling them the FUNNIEST
thing EVER. I had to write it down.
So get this... Avril, who's said nothing for
the entire journey and most of the evening
too, only ...

TALKS IN HER SLEEP!

"She's having **WHOLE** conversations and won't STOP.

What am I going to do?"

Mum and Dad must have suggested she sleep in the front room because I can HEAR her dragging blankets to the sofa. (I wonder what **Avril** has been talking about?)

Ha! Ha!

That would annoy her a LOT.

So the thing is, Delia, I think that your brother Tom is very smart.

Date	DAY TWO	
Weather	Rain (but thinner)	**My Plans for the Day**
Mood	Tired 😐	More sleep. Find out what Avril talks about in her sleep.

Dear Diary,

I'm a bit tired this morning (thanks to **Avril** and Delia). After unpacking my bag I've also discovered that Mum hasn't brought ANYTHING I wanted. No guitar, none of my odd stone collection, and WORSE STILL, none of my nice pens, <u>AND</u> I've only got <u>ONE</u> pair of PANTS. How did that happen after Mum kept reminding <u>ME?</u> Maybe they're in another bag. I'll have to ask.

(Great.)

Everyone looked a bit tired (apart from Avril).

I mentioned my PANTS situation to Mum quietly.

She said, "Sorry, Tom, I don't know how that

happened."

(I do! She FORGOT THEM.)

Mum asked Avril if she slept OK and she said,

YES, as if nothing had happened.

So I said, "Avril, is it true you talk in

your sleep?"

NO, she said, like I'd asked the

STUPIDEST question EVER.

"But Delia said..." I started to say when Delia

NUDGED me and whispered,

"Shhhh! She doesn't KNOW she does it!"

Shhhh!

What?

Mum gave me a LOOK too.

So I kept QUIET.

Dad wanted to tell us his PLANS for the day.
"Listen, everyone, this VILLA might
not be perfect, but WE'RE on
HOLIDAY, so LET'S make the MOST of it
and GO and EXPLORE the area."
Delia wasn't impressed (especially after her
night on the sofa).

"EXPLORE? You said we're on
holiday – what happened to RELAXING?
AND it's STILL raining." Which was true.

Mum suggested we could drive to the
nearest TOWN and have a look around.

"We're not SHOPPING, are we?"
I asked, because that's what it sounded like.

"Not necessarily, but we could get you
some more  PANTS ."

Brilliant.

Mum was talking about my pants again, and in front of **Avril** and Delia – who said it
 was "gross".

Then Mum told us, "Your dad's  RIGHT – we <u>should</u> make the most of our time here together. EVEN if this villa is a bit grotty, and nothing works, and the electrics flicker on and off, and the rooms are tiny – apart from yours, Delia and **Avril**. At least it looks like the RAIN is easing up at last."

As soon as Mum said that, the ceiling in the kitchen started to LEAK. I helped put the plastic containers under the drips.

"Lucky I brought so many," Mum sighed.

Dad said, "Enough's enough – let's see if
we can SWAP "villas".
Which cheered Mum up. Delia and **Avril**
disappeared back to "their" room and Mum
kept the leaks under control while Dad walked
around trying to get a signal for his phone.
I kept myself busy by:
Writing stuff in my DIARY   (like this).
Watching the RAIN. Drawing the RAIN.
I EVEN wrote a RAIN poem in the SHAPE of a
RAINDROP.

It's
RAINING
It's pouring
This weather
IS BORING
If it doesn't get
I'm BETTER
going to get
WETTER.

Here's my view out of the window.

Draw a NICER view here!

Mum's plastic container →

NEXT ↓

I found some EMPTY water bottles and had a game of WATER Bottle Skittles to pass the time.

How to make and play SKITTLEs with plastic bottles (Good for rainy days)

Take some empty plastic bottles that are roughly the same size. Check the lids FIT nicely (get a grown-up to help if you need to). Then fill them with enough water so they're STURDY, but not too tricky to knock down.

You can use a STICKY NOTE or paper and sticky tape to add NUMBERS on to the bottles.

These are POINTS SCORED when the bottles are knocked down.

Use a scrunched-up ball of FOIL as a ball – or something soft if you're playing inside.

You can use some bottles with no water to make them easier to knock down.

Decide how far away to stand and put down a MARKER of some kind so everyone stands the same distance away.

Then PLAY!

Yes!

Knocking all the bottles down is a

STRIKE

and is very impressive.

Dear Diary,

This is a BIN BAG (on a roll).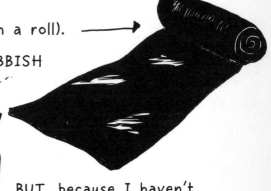

Usually people put RUBBISH

in bin bags,

LIKE THIS.

BUT, because I haven't

got a raincoat (or ANY coat), Mum decided

it would be a GOOD idea to make me a RAIN

cape out of a <u>BIN</u> <u>BAG</u>.

"It will keep you dry when we go out," she said.

"No thanks! I'd rather get WET than

wear a BIN BAG," I told her.

"We might have to walk in the POURING

rain - you'll get SOAKED!"

(I still wasn't convinced.)

"No one will SEE you..." Mum told me.

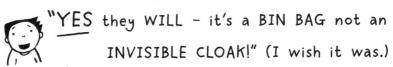

"YES they WILL - it's a BIN BAG not an

INVISIBLE CLOAK!" (I wish it was.)

"NO one that you KNOW will see you.

And it won't be for long. We need to

go into town to get you some PANTS.

(Mum said pants AGAIN.)

Then she added... "AND a nice TREAT."

So I put it on.

"There, that's not bad, is it?" Mum said

while adjusting the hood.

"WHY is Tom wearing a BIN BAG?"

Delia asked. (She ALWAYS turns up

at the WRONG time.)

Avril just STARED at me.

"It's a RAIN CAPE," I told her.

"It's a BIN BAG," Delia said again.

"You can't tell it's a bin bag though,"

Mum tried to convince us.

"Errr ... YES you can," Delia said, smirking.

"I don't care because I'm getting a TREAT,"

I said like that made a difference.

"I hope your treat is better that your BIN BAG,"

Delia LAUGHED.

I was about to take off the ~~bin bag~~ –
RAIN cape – when Dad came charging
in and told us we weren't going
ANYWHERE.

"The car's SUNK into a BIG puddle.
It's STUCK. Rita, you drive and WE'LL
give the car a good *PUSH.*"

"We're not standing in the RAIN
getting WET,"
Delia complained.

"Make a RAIN CAPE, then," I suggested.

"And look ridiculous? No thanks."

"Come on, Delia – we ALL need to help.
If you want us to go OUT, let's get this car
moving," Dad said.

Reluctantly Delia and Avril put their jackets
over their heads and followed us out to the car
(in the rain). "Call this a holiday..." she muttered.

Mum started the engine and tried to get the car to move. But nothing happened.

Stuck

So we stood at the back of the car and Dad said, "OK, on the count of THREE we'll all push.

READY? ONE ... TWO ... THREE...

PUSH!"

As we pushed, Mum REALLY REVVED the engine UP!
And the wheels spun round...

A LOT

The car was still STUCK, but at least I managed
to AVOID most of the mud.
(Thanks to my rain cape — and Dad.)

"THIS IS THE WORST HOLIDAY EVER!" Delia said
dramatically. Avril agreed. I think.

(It was hard to tell under all the mud.)

"I don't look so ridiculous NOW!" I couldn't resist saying as they went back to the villa, dripping mud along the way.

The car wasn't going anywhere and neither were we.

"I think I'll have to go and find some HELP," said Dad.

"Good idea, but maybe change out of the muddy clothes first?" Mum replied, still tipping rainwater from the plastic containers.

"Obviously!" Dad said.

(I just had to take off my rain cape.)

Clean

It looked like we'd be here for a while, and thanks to Mum's lack of packing (NOT bringing ANY of my STUFF 😔), I thought I'd see what else was around the villa.

Under a bookcase was a cupboard and inside I discovered a few interesting things.

A pack of cards (some missing).

A box of board games (with only snakes and ladders, one dice and no counters).

An old telescope and a map of the STARS (stars in the sky – not celebrities).

A few books by someone called Mills and Boon.

AND two sets of KEYS, which I gave to Mum. She was really happy because BOTH sets worked in the front door (unlike like the ones we had). 🙂

I showed her the other stuff I'd found and
Mum asked if I wanted to play a game which
was *BRILLIANT.*

"That's the good thing about holidays,"
Mum said as she got out some different coins
from her purse. "There's LOTS
more time to do things like THIS."
She put the coins down to use as counters.

I was the POUND and she was the penny.
We were about to throw the dice when
we heard Dad YELP from the shower.

There's NO hot water LEFT!

Mum LAUGHED and told him it was good
practice for surfing in the cold sea! I WON
two out of three games of snakes and ladders.
AND after that Mum got out some foil and
showed me ...

Take a roll of FOIL and tear
or cut three strips off. Be careful
or ask an adult if you're using scissors.

Fold one strip over and over
to make a thin but THICK leg.

You can
SCRUNCH

them as you go to make them rounder.

LIKE THIS
↓

Now do the same with the
OTHER leg.

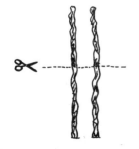

When you have two legs
together, cut them in the
middle so you have FOUR legs
the same length.

Put the legs on top of each other in a sort of STAR SHAPE. Then hold them in the centre and gently TWIST the legs together a little.

This makes it easier to make the spider body.

Once you've got your legs, use the other strip of foil to WRAP around the centre of the legs to make a body.

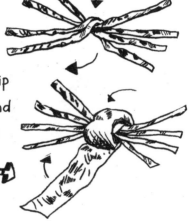

KEEP adding strips of foil and PUSH down the sides to make it into a SPIDER SHAPE until it's the size you want.

Like this

Then gently bend the legs up into a SPIDER SHAPE.

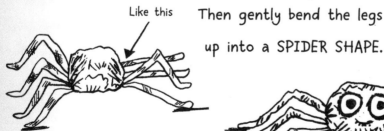

You can paint your spider all over – OR just paint on some EYES.

A spider

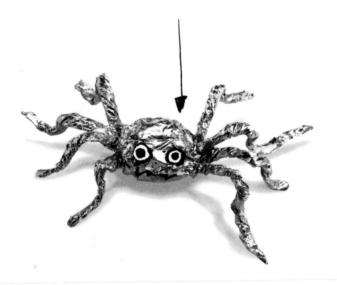

It's amazing what you can do to entertain yourself when you're stuck inside for a long time...

Sorry about my family. You never know what they're going to do next.

Ewww.

Date	DAY THREE	
Weather	Clouds. Still Raining	**My Plans for the Day**
Mood	Hopeful	BEACH if it stops raining (it hasn't). ☺

Dear Diary,

THIS was the FIRST thing that I saw when I went to the bathroom this morning.

MY PANTS hanging over the shower rail.

They'd been WASHED, which would have been OK – IF they were DRY.

(They weren't.)

AND as they're my ONLY pair, I had to put on DAMP pants ...

... Which was uncomfortable at first, until they warmed up.

Delia spent the night on the sofa (again) thanks to Avril's SLEEP TALKING.

Surprisingly she didn't seem too grumpy about it (unlike yesterday).

I think it's because Delia and Avril went to the PINE TREE RIVIERA CLUBHOUSE last night.

They found a map showing where it was and told Mum and Dad,

"We're going out to find SOME LIFE ..."

I said "I'll come with you."

Because a CLUBHOUSE sounded like fun.

"I don't think so - not after your spider tricks."

(At least it worked.)

Mum said, "We'll all join you later, Delia." and she looked THRILLED about THAT news.

(Avril looked the same.)

FINALLY Dad got a phone signal and spoke to the villa owners who were surprised we weren't

Hello! Hello!

Bin bag.

happy and told Dad it was one of their BEST villas.

"I'd hate to see the others!" Mum said.

Dad told us they'd agreed

What a relief!

we can swap, which is good news.

Delia and **Avril** were waiting to go out,

so Mum made them PROMISE to:

☆ BE sensible.

☆ BE polite. ⟵ Tricky

★ Take the spare keys.

★ Take spare bin bags in case it rained.

(Again).

Reluctantly, Delia stuffed a couple into her bag — then asked for some money as well.

I WAVED **goodbye...**

BYE

and they ignored me.

Half an hour later we left to join them.

I was really hungry and looking

forward to seeing the Pine Tree Riviera

CLUBHOUSE 🌲 for myself.

(THAT was the [PLAN,] but as usual

things didn't quite work out.)

"Are we lost?" I asked,

after the THIRD time we'd

walked in a CIRCLE.

"It can't be *TOO* far away – Delia always says she

doesn't 'do' walking," Dad told us.

I could SMELL FOOD,

which was making me really hungry.

"We'll get there eventually," Mum said.

"The CLUBHOUSE must be around here somewhere."

After another TWENTY minutes it began to

rain HEAVILY.

"OK, I give up," Dad said.

So we all went back to the villa.

Bin bags

"What happened to you lot then?" Delia asked when they finally got home.

"Dad got lost," I told them.

"It was a HARD place to FIND!" he protested.
"WHERE WERE YOU?"

"In the CLUBHOUSE, like we said."

(Which wasn't much help.)

🌲 SO TONIGHT we're going to the clubhouse with Delia, Avril and MOST IMPORTANTLY ▬▷ THE MAP. The rain's almost stopped and the GOOD NEWS is the MUD PUDDLE around the car has nearly gone too.

Dad thinks we can free the car and even ... go to the BEACH.

Yeah! The BEACH!

I said, jumping up and down.

Delia didn't want to come with us, which I thought was **WEIRD.** <u>WHO</u> doesn't like the BEACH? It's more fun than staying inside. 〝〞

"Are you two sure? We're having a picnic," Mum said, like THAT would make a difference.

"It's just going to RAIN again. BESIDES, we want to go to the CLUBHOUSE. If we can have some more ... money?" she added.

(I had to admire how Delia slipped that in.) Dad reminded us we were swapping to a NICER villa this afternoon. "So no more leaky CEILINGS, I hope!" he said as a BIG DRIP hit my head.

Huh?

194

The BEST part of Delia and Avril not
coming to the beach with us was
getting my OLD seat back.  Yes
Before Dad loaded the picnic box
into the boot, Mum said, "Let's check
the car's not still STUCK, shall we?" Which seemed
like a good idea. Just in case, Dad and I stood a
SAFE MUD-FREE distance away. (It worked.)

We jumped in the
car and followed the
signs for the beach,
which was EASY to find and NOT too far
away. The beach looked really nice - until we got
out of the car...

"At least it's WARM WIND..." Dad said.

(It wasn't

THAT warm.)

There were a few people surfing in the sea already.

We battled our way down to find a nice place to set up. Sand kept flicking up in my FACE so I put on some goggles while Mum weighed the towels down with stones. "Mind how you sit on them," she told me.

Dad tried to get changed, which is always tricky on a WINDY BEACH.

"Come on, Tom – LET'S go!" he said enthusiastically.

"Be careful, won't you?" shouted Mum.

"We will! I'm a natural surfer," Dad laughed.

And off we went...

Dad

BEFORE

Dad

AFTER

He lasted about TWO minutes before he lost his balance and got TUMBLED over by a wave. Some kids helped him up and kept hold of his board.

"Maybe I need a wetsuit?" Dad said as he got out.

I spent more time than Dad in the sea and only got out when my fingers started to turn blue (it was a bit cold). Dad was telling Mum that the wave was ENORMOUS as she tried to put a plaster on his nose. (It wasn't.) At least we managed to eat our sandwiches before the WIND and sand flew up and ruined our picnic.

"Good job I put them in plastic boxes," Mum said. I was about to go rock-pooling when the clouds gathered and it began to POUR with rain (AGAIN). We only just made it back to the car in time.

Date	DAY FOUR	
Weather	Not great	**My Plans for the Day**
Mood	Started OK	No more bin bags. EVER.

Dear Diary,

Even though it rained yesterday, I LOVED going to the beach. It felt more like a holiday.

But THAT was YESTERDAY morning.

What happened in the afternoon was possibly the MOST embarrassing moment in my WHOLE

LIFE.  (So far.)

As it was pouring with rain Mum and Dad decided it was a good time to go into town and pick up more supplies.

 "AND some PANTS for you," Mum added.

So I reminded them about the TREAT they'd

promised me as well

(which was FAR more important). 🙂

Dad found the town centre and the SHOPS. It was

really busy and there was NOWHERE

to park. He kept driving around

until eventually Mum spotted a space.

(Quick! Grab it!) she YELLED. So after

a few goes Dad parked

the car. It was quite a long way to walk back to

the shops (and the RAIN was still ~~heavy~~ too).

"Don't worry, Tom – I have more bin

bags so you won't have to get WET."

I put it on and just thought about my TREAT.

(Sigh.)

We found the clothes shop quite *quickly* and LUCKILY the BOYS' section was near the door. The WHOLE place was packed. I didn't want to stay too long (neither did Dad). I was about to take off my rain cape when Mum held up some BOYS' PANTS and started saying REALLY LOUDLY,

"WILL THESE FIT? WHAT SIZE PANTS DO YOU TAKE, TOM?"

I wanted to hide. So I kept my rain cape on while Mum waved PANTS around like they were FLAGS.

"Which ones do you like?
BOXERS, Y-FRONTS, STRIPES or these

SUPERHERO PANTS

are ☆FUN☆!"

"I'd like a pair of
SUPERHERO PANTS please!"
Dad joined in.

It was ALL getting a bit much.

There was Dad with his dodgy nose and plaster.

Mum holding up PANTS.

And me wearing a bin bag while trying to hide so no one could see my very embarrassed FACE.

Or that's what I thought.

Until someone tapped me on the shoulder and said,

"Is THAT you, Tom?"

THE **LAST PERSON**
I EXPECTED TO SEE WAS
AMY PORTER.

"Are you wearing a bin bag?" she asked me.
I managed to mutter "Hello" and something about
it being a "long story" in a very
embarrassed way. But at least it stopped Mum
from talking about PANTS.

AMY'S mum was there too, and it turned out
they were staying at the PINE TREE RIVIERA
as well – only in a really NICE villa (not like ours).

All this talk about villas reminded Dad we were supposed to be MOVING to a new one.

"We better get back," he pointed out, which was a HUGE relief for me.

As we headed out into the rain (again) AMY said, "I might see you at the CLUBHOUSE then, Tom?"

"If we can find it," I told her, still feeling awkward.

I didn't even mind about NOT getting a TREAT because I was just happy to

leave QUICKLY.

Bin bag cape

Mum and Dad were still discussing whose idea it was to book PINE TREE RIVIERA in the first place on the drive back.

"How did AMY'S Mum get a nice villa - and we didn't?"

"That's a good question," Dad said.

(I kept quiet. I still can't believe AMY is here.)

When we got back there was no sign of the villa owners or Delia and Avril.

They'd left a NOTE that said,

Gone to the clubhouse.

See you later.
(Maybe.)

(She'd used one of my STICKY NOTES, which was annoying.)

Dad called up the owners and I heard him say:

"YES, HELLO, it's Frank GATES. Where? I can't see you. I'm HERE, where are YOU? It doesn't look like the villa I booked. Right now, please. Thank you."

Then Dad told us to "PACK UP – they're coming to MOVE us right now."

Mum said, "AT LAST!"

It didn't take long to shove all my stuff back in my bag, so while they talked about whose FAULT it was (again), I remembered the old telescope I'd found. Now seemed like a good time to use it.

I took it to the back of the villa and looked through the window in the bathroom.

At first, I couldn't see much. Then in the distance, through a G A P in the trees I saw something that looked like ...

THE CLUBHOUSE

The CLUBHOUSE

PINE TREE RIV

I focused the telescope. It WAS the CLUBHOUSE. How could we have missed it?

(It was so close.)

As I kept watching two people who looked VERY familiar stepped on to the small stage.

I ADJUSTED the telescope again, as it was a bit cracked, to make sure I wasn't SEEING things.

And THERE...

... I spotted...

Delia and Avril SINGING!

They **EVEN** seemed to be enjoying themselves, which was confusing. I wanted to keep watching them but Mum and Dad started calling me and saying we had to go.

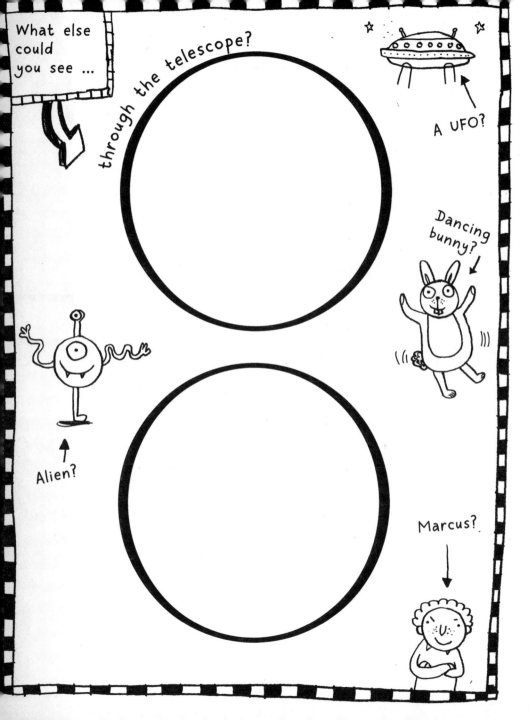

What else could you see ...

through the telescope?

A UFO?

Dancing bunny?

Alien?

Marcus?

I wanted to tell Mum and Dad about Delia and **Avril**, but I didn't get a CHANCE.
They were already packed

and telling me to **HuRRY uP!**

BECAUSE ALL this **TIME** we've been staying in

THE WRONG PLACE

Apparently the PINE TREE RIVIERA moved to a new site last year and somehow we ended up on the old one. Mum and Dad couldn't believe it when the owners told them that!

"You mean we're in the wrong villa?"

(We were.)

After that surprise we got in our car and followed the owners to our NEW VILLA, which was SO much nicer.

"It looks like the pictures!" I told Mum and Dad, which was a GOOD thing. ☺

The owners wondered HOW we'd managed to get into the OLD villa with the wrong set of keys? I could tell Mum and Dad didn't want me to mention my NINJA jumping and window-climbing skills.

So I kept quiet.

Anyway, it didn't matter NOW ... because I had a BIGGER ROOM, even if it was only for ONE night and we could see the CLUBHOUSE as well. Mum said we'd better let Delia and Avril know where we'd gone.

"They're SINGING OVER THERE," I told them, pointing to the CLUBHOUSE.

"I SAW them."

Dad looked puzzled.

"Singing? Are you SURE? I must see this," Dad said.

But by the time he got to the CLUBHOUSE, they'd already stopped. So he brought them to the new villa instead.

Sweet...

"I can't believe we messed up the villas!" Mum said.

"I can," replied Delia.

Mum changed the subject and asked what the CLUBHOUSE was LIKE. "We'll all have to go there TONIGHT!" she added.

"It's BORING. You won't like it. Don't go there," Delia told them QUICKLY.

So I said, "You two seemed to be enjoying yourselves SINGING when I saw you through my telescope!"

For a second Delia was speechless.
(Avril didn't say much either.)

Huh?

I thought **AMY** seeing me wear a BIN BAG was embarrassing but compared to what happened later that was NOTHING...

LATER

Somehow, Mum managed to persuade Delia and **Avril** to come with us to the CLUBHOUSE (now we could find it).

"It's our LAST CHANCE – we'll have a GREAT time. You can show us your singing SKILLS!" she said.

La!

La! La! La! La!

(Me demonstrating Delia and Avril singing)

"I've SEEN them singing already," I laughed. Ha! Ha!

"That wasn't us. You're talking Nonsense,

Delia grumbled.

(Which wasn't TRUE and I was about to PROVE it.)

When we got to the CLUBHOUSE I pointed to all the KARAOKE posters everywhere – including a KARAOKE CHART that was on the wall.

"LOOK! Delia and Avril are at NUMBER THREE!" I shouted really LOUDLY!

(They'd been rumbled.)

"All right, Tom – we had to find something to DO.

It was a ONE-OFF – wasn't it, Avril?"

Avril nodded.

* * TOP * * KARAOKE CHART	
1	☆ PIP ☆
2	✦CHRIS✦
3	AVRIL & DELIA
4	★ ALI ☆
5	VICKY

"Can we JUST order some food?" Delia sighed.

Which wasn't such a BAD idea. 😊

While we were eating Dad spotted something VERY

interesting.

"Look, Tom – the prize for tonight's is a

family ticket to CHOCOLATE WORLD. Shall

we have a go?" (I was almost tempted.)

"Count me in," Mum said cheerfully.

"Count us out," Delia added.

Dad put down our names and I thought of

chocolate and (eventually) agreed to sing a song by

the BEATLES.

(Thanks to Mr Fingle, I've heard loads of OLD

BANDS and know a lot of their songs.)

The only trouble was, when it was our turn to go

up and choose, instead of pressing the button for

"LET IT BE"

Mum got confused and pressed...

This one?

Huh?

Delia and Avril left halfway through the second verse, but everyone ELSE seemed to like our singing and we even got a BIG round of applause at the end.

Which almost made up for the SHAME of doing family KARAOKE with your mum and dad.

I was just glad it was all OVER.

(No more embarrassing moments.)

Then I noticed someone at the BACK was

WAVING at ME. ⬇

WHY DID IT HAVE TO BE AMY PORTER?

Now she'd seen me singing "Let It Go" with my
overenthusiastic parents – and wearing a BIN BAG.
I just hoped she wouldn't tell too many people at
school about ... well, ANYTHING.

This page is for you to draw <u>whatever</u>.

(It's a DISTRACTION page.)

Date	DAY FIVE	
Weather	Sunny	**My Plans for the Day**
Mood	Perky	So many (when I get home).

Dear Diary,

I LIKE holidays – and this one had its ☆FUN☆

moments. (Some...)

As soon as we packed up the car and left

PINE TREE RIVIERA, the clouds disappeared

and the SUN ☼ came out.

"That's TYPICAL," Mum sighed as we drove off.

It's hard to tell if **Avril** enjoyed herself.

She didn't say much on the journey home.

Delia announced this was the

LAST TIME she would ever come on

holiday with us.

Bye. Thanks.

I said  Just to CHECK

if she meant it.

(As Derek could definitely come with us next time.)

Mum said, "We'll see – you're not

quite old enough to be left alone." Mum with sunglasses

Which Delia wasn't happy about at all. She started

to REMIND them about EVERYTHING that had gone

WRONG. "So I can find the CLUBHOUSE and

you can't, but I'm not old enough to be on my own?"

 "That's right, Delia..."

"But that's NOT FAIR!"

They started to have an ARGUMENT until Dad broke

into SONG to stop them.

 he sung...

Which seemed to work.

(Though it did remind me of my singing shame...)

Sigh.

Right now

I'm VERY happy to be back in my

OWN HOME, in my

OWN ROOM, with my

OWN STUFF

Comics
Pens
Snacks

(and all the things that Mum didn't pack.)

I'm not so happy to see THIS.

(The folder and worksheets I still

have to do for school.)

I've got a few days left – there's NO hurry.

So I decide the MOST important thing to do

FIRST is ...

Tell Derek I'm **BACK** with some STICKY NOTE messages on my window.

HI DEREK | I'm BACK | DOG | ZOMB | IES

BA | ND | PR | ACT | ICE | soon? | Let's go for CHEESY

AND THIS ONE goes on my DOOR

(for obvious reasons).

KEEP OUT!

No one who wears

sunglasses allowed.

(You know who you are.)

		DAY ~~SIX~~ Seven	
Weather	Raining (again)	**Plans for the Day**	
Mood	CHILLED 😊	BAND PRACTICE	

Dear Diary,

Sorry I forgot to write anything yesterday, but I was too busy having FUN.

On a HOLIDAY METER, our trip to

PINE TREE RIVIERA ended up being around HERE

I'm hoping when I get back to school AMY PORTER

will keep my singing skills to herself ...

.... or it might drop back to GRIM!

I never did get the **TREAT** Mum promised me. SO AFTER A FEW HINTS I've got some nice things for the **DOGZOMBIES** band practice.

I had to put a NOTE on my WAFERS to keep my FAMILY AWAY. (Dad had been hovering around looking hungry.)

Oooh, wafers!

It did the TRICK and kept them SAFE until I took them to Derek's – along with the OTHER snacks I'd saved.

We had a good STASH now.

So the first thing we did was **DIVIDE** all the treats up between us. (Which took a while.)

Then we spent the next TWO HOURS practising **DOGZOMBIES** TUNES and talking about music, until Derek stood up and SHOUTED ...

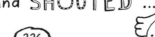

YES!

We cheered and jumped around the room, until Derek's dad came in and told us all to

Quiet down, boys...

So we did.

DOGZOMBIES Hooray.

(We're going to work on THAT PLAN for sure... WATCH this space.)

Date	DAY ~~SEVEN~~ Eight	
Weather	Rain (again)	**My Plans for the Day**
Mood	PANIC 	TRY NOT TO PANIC

𝔻ear 𝔻iary,

This morning the **RAIN** and thunder woke me up.

Which was annoying. (I had enough of BAD

WEATHER on holiday.) AND THEN I spotted my

FOLDER STUFFED `FuLL` of

worksheets still.

With all my band practice and distractions (snacks),

I'd forgotten to finish them off.

I was thinking WHAT am I going to do? BUT

THEN I remembered

 My <u>LIST</u> of
HOMEWORK ...

EXCUSES!

(Brilliant! I KNEW it would come in handy!)

I took a good LOOK ➜ and ONE

excuse LEAPT out at me.

(NOT the alien one this time.)

So I walked to school in the POURING RAIN

and my folder made an EXCELLENT umbrella to keep

ME dry. Sadly ALL my worksheets got

SOAKING **WET** and were completely

RuINED! (Oh no ... DISASTER!) ☺

Mr Fullerman didn't let me off the hook

completely. He gave me a STERN LOOK,

a new set of worksheets and a tiny bit

more time to finish them off.

Which was better than nothing.

Whoops

Marcus thought I was lucky.

Then he said something that I REALLY

wasn't expecting...

"HEY, Tom - I've got something for you!"

 "REALLY? Thanks Marcus," I said.

Then he lifted up his school bag and behind it was a BAR of chocolate from CHOCOLATE WORLD!

"WOW - is THAT for me?" I asked.

(Even Amy looked surprised.)

"Yes, Tom -

it's ALL for YOU."

Marcus smiled.

So I went to pick it up ...

... and of COURSE it was empty.

Marcus couldn't stop LAUGHING at his JOKE.

Ha! Ha! Ha! Ha!
Ha! Ha! HA! HA!

It started to get annoying after half an hour.

Sigh... So I used one of my LAST sticky NOTES to write a little message.

When AMY nudged me and said,

"Do you know WHAT you should really do NOW, Tom?"

"What's that AMY ?" I asked.

"Just let it go!" She LAUGHED. "You weren't bad – and it was FUNNY!" she added, which kind of made it less embarrassing.

"Actually, AMY, THIS is WHAT I should do." Then I put my super good ninja skills ...

.... to very good use once again.

With some of my STICKY NOTES
I make a FLIP book* HERE'S HOW:

Decide what you want to draw on a rough piece of paper first. (Try something simple to begin with!) Here's how to do Mr Fullerman's face with BEADY EYES.

1 2 3 4 5 6 7 8

In the corner of each note, starting at the back, draw your first face.

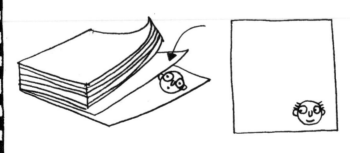

Then on the second note, TRACE over the face and move the eyes and mouth slightly – like picture 2.

Keep adding the drawings and moving the eyes around on every NOTE.

It does take a WHILE, but when you've drawn on quite a few, FLICK through the book to see how he's moving. The more pictures you draw, the better it will work.

Here's some other ideas to try:
A STICK MAN jumping.

     Delia being hit by mud!

*See Tom Gates: Genius Ideas (mostly) for a BUG flipbook in the corner.

A
Annoying
Delia

B
Brilliant
band

C
Champ
expert

D
Doodling
skills

J
Jumping
very HIGH

K
Keeping a
very straight
face

L
Laughing at
Dad's bad
jokes

M
Making STUF
(like a
kite skill)

Q
Quiz expert
(TRUE)

R
Running
skill

S
Singing in
my band

T
Teaching
Rooster
to
dance

X
X_RAY EYES (I don't
have this - but it
would be good)

Y
Yodelling
(Thanks to
Ms Yodel)

Z
Zoning out
but still awake
(just)

E

Expert at
balancing stuff

← wafers

F

Face
tune
skills

G

Guitar
skills

H

Hiding my
sisters
sunglasses

I

Ink blob
monster
skills

N

Ninja skills

O

Orange
fruit doodle

P

Poem Skill
You know I will have
lots of skills. I'm a poet
Don't you know it.

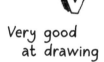

U

Unusual string
doodles

V

Very good
at drawing

W

Wafer
biscuit
trick skill

Here's an ALPHABET of MY

very own SUPER GOOD SKILLS

(I have MANY. . . sort of).

Here's a random page for you to draw on (Enjoy)

True or False - Answers...

		TRUE	FAL
1	False – it is a bird.		X
2	False – they grow from the ground.		X
3	True – a spider does have eight legs.	X	
4	False – you get GREEN.		X
5	False – they are made-up creatures.		X
6	False – it's Canberra.		X
7	True – honey is made by bees.	X	
8	True – But they died out and became extinct.	X	
9	True – red and yellow make orange.	X	
10	False – the cheetah is the fastest animal.		X

... And the answers to the ones I made up

	TRUE	FALSE
False – his dog is tiny.		X
False – she has a BIT of a moustache.		X
True – (no question.)	X	
True – caramel wafers are delicious.	X	
False – they LOVE scary films.		X
False – although he thinks he does.		X
True – they're BEADY too.	X	
True – all my photos are tragic.	X	
False – she's always grumpy when I see her.		X
True – he shares his sweets too.	X	

When Liz 🖼 was little Ω, she loved to draw, paint and make things. Her mum used to say she was very good at making a mess (which is still true today!).

She kept drawing and went to art school, where she earned a degree in graphic design. She worked as a designer and art director in the music industry 🎸, and her freelance work has appeared on a wide variety of products.

Liz is the author-illustrator of several picture books. Tom Gates is the first series of books she has written and illustrated for older children. They have won several prestigious awards ⭐, including the Roald Dahl Funny Prize, the Waterstones Children's Book Prize, and the Blue Peter Book Award. The books have been translated into forty-one languages worldwide.

Visit her at www.LizPichon.com

Keep your BEADY EYES open for the other hilarious TOM GATES books!

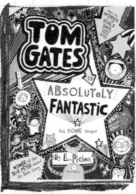

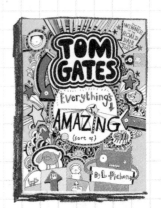

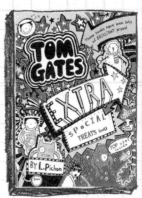

So many

For more news about Liz Pichon
and the Tom Gates books, go to: Lizpichon.com

AND to Scholastic's fantastic Tom Gates
website:www.scholastic.co.uk/tomgatesworld